He stood beside the line of graves while Tonto held Silver and Scout. Now there was one more grave—his own.

He took a deep breath and stared at the ground. "Let Cavendish and all men think that I died here with the Rangers."

"Dan," he said, kneeling beside his brother's grave. "I'll see that your boy is well taken care of as long as I am alive. And I swear to you, wherever your murderers are, however long it takes, I *will* find them. What Cavendish and men like him owe you, they will pay in full. *To this I pledge my life!*"

He stood, placed his hat back on and slowly turned to face his Indian friend. He wore a black leather mask, soaked wet with his own tears and Captain Dan Reid's blood.

Tonto shivered and stared in awe at the Lone Ranger.

LORD GRADE and JACK WRATHER

Present

A MARTIN STARGER PRODUCTION

"THE LEGEND OF THE LONE RANGER"

Starring
KLINTON SPILSBURY, MICHAEL HORSE,
CHRISTOPHER LLOYD

MATT CLARK, and introducing JUANIN CLAY

and

JASON ROBARDS as
PRESIDENT ULYSSES S. GRANT

Executive Producer MARTIN STARGER
Original music by JOHN BARRY
Director of Photography LASZLO KOVACS, A.S.C.

Screenplay by
IVAN GOFF & BEN ROBERTS and
MICHAEL KANE and WILLIAM ROBERTS

Adaptation by JERRY DERLOSHON

Produced by WALTER COBLENZ

Directed by WILLIAM FRAKER

— An AFD/UNIVERSAL Release —

THE
Legend
OF THE
Lone Ranger

A Novel by Gary McCarthy

Based on the screenplay by
Ivan Goff & Ben Roberts and
Michael Kane and William Roberts
and the adaptation by Jerry Derloshon

BALLANTINE BOOKS • NEW YORK

Library of Congress Catalog Card Number: 80-68214

ISBN 0-345-29438-6

Manufactured in the United States of America

First Edition: June 1981

Chapter 1

THE eleven-year-old Indian boy, stretched flat on the back of his pony, hugged it tightly as deadly, searching bullets flew overhead. The distance between the Indian and the outlaws narrowed with each pounding of hooves. He could feel his pony's legs falter, beginning to lose their swiftness. He clutched at the horse's mane, his lean young body straining to feed the animal his own strength and spirit, urging the pony toward the mountains—and safety.

The Indian boy's long hair, black as raven feathers, streamed out behind him. Fear and determination shone in his youthful face. These men, whom he'd chanced upon moments earlier while hunting rabbit, were now hunting their own game. They were after his scalp and would brag of how they'd won it with honor while they sold his pony in the white man's settlements.

A bullet sliced across his naked thigh and the boy ground his teeth as the warm blood flowed down his leg. He was an Indian warrior about to die—strong, impassive, fearless.

His pony leapt into a small, dry streambed and struggled up the opposite bank. He could hear it gasping desperately for air. Another mile, maybe two, and the valiant pony's heart would explode like a bullet in a campfire.

In that desperate moment, the Indian knew he had to fight like a warrior instead of dying like a rabbit chased by coyotes.

A bullet seared across his pony's haunches and the animal screamed its pain. Somehow it found the last depths of its strength and raced blindly onward. The boy reached over his shoulder, groping for the small hunting bow and arrows. His nimble brown fingers plucked an arrow from his quiver and fitted it smoothly into the notch as he sat up straight on the pony's back.

His eyes searched desperately for a small outcropping of rocks where he could throw himself off the animal and make his last stand. The thin trail he followed stretched like a dead snake through this high brush country. He realized his only chance lay in cutting straight across and back toward the riverbed. His knees were tensed, steering the pony into the chaparral, and he felt the sharp, burning pain in his right leg.

"Get that red bastard! He's cutting off the trail. Don't let him get back to the arroyo!"

"Shoot his pony, goddammit! Ain't nothin' but a runt anyway!"

The boy understood their words, and fear and hatred burned deep into his heart. He'd run out of time and the end was near. As long as they'd shot only for his body, he had a chance, but if they got his brave pony . . .

A bullet scooped a hunk of flesh and mane into the boy's face. Through the blood and tears he whispered, "Goodbye, my friend," before everything plunged into darkness.

"I got him! I sure as hell got him in the back!

Did you see him jackknife up like his backbone snapped?"

"Hell, yes. But where's his body? We can get six bits for Indian scalps down at the traders."

The Indian boy stirred, feeling the ground shake as the outlaws pushed their horses through the heavy undergrowth. They were close, swearing and yelling things he did not understand. His hand felt for the bow, and his heart soared to find it within his reach. But he would never have a chance to use it in the high brush. Better the hunting knife!

A hand gripped his wrist and he tried to tear the knife from his belt, but the fall had left him too weak and shaken. He looked up and saw a white boy. A strong boy, with eyes that pleaded for silence.

"He's gotta be in here someplace!"

"Well, then you find him. I'm sick of wasting my time here. We never shoulda left the others and took off after that little red bastard. Let's get back and have us some real fun. Might even kill the man and use his woman!"

"What about the pony?"

"You want him?"

"Hell, yeah. Ain't big, but he sure can run. I'll throw a rope on him."

The Indian struggled to get up, but the white boy held him.

"My name is John Reid and, if you want to live, you'd better stay down!" he commanded, pulling his arm up behind his back. "And keep still!"

"Goddam Indian pony won't let me get close enough to rope!"

His partner laughed. "It's your smell. Hell, I wouldn't come either. He ain't dumb."

"Oh, yeah!" The voice was thick with anger. "Well, it sure ain't smart."

The unmistakable cocking of a rifle made the young Indian go wild, then rigid as stone when the rifle boomed.

"Goddamit, you only nicked him! Won't stop running until he gets to Mexico. Let's ride back to that house before we miss out on all the fun."

John Reid was only a boy, but he was sinewy and tough from doing a man's work, helping his mother and father eke out a living on their hard-scrabble Texas land. His father always claimed that John was worth two ordinary cowhands when it came to handling cattle or chopping firewood. But John knew he might have met his match in the Indian. The kid exploded with savagery, bucking at the weight on his back and silently fighting to gain the advantage. John held on, knowing that if the Indian got up now, he might have to kill him or be killed himself.

"Hold still," John pleaded. "I don't want to hurt you!"

The Indian calmed down and, in clean, cold English, said, "Let me up, son of a white man. Let me up and I will show you how a warrior fights."

"I don't *want* to see you fight," John said with exasperation.

"Then you are a coward!"

John swallowed hard. He *wasn't* a coward. A coward would never have interfered. He could have stayed put at the hidden spring up in the rocks.

"I'm no coward," he gritted. "Not like those two who chased you down and shot at your horse."

"There were four," the Indian snapped.

John's grip tightened and his mind flashed back to the conversation he'd heard but not really listened to, while he'd been trying to subdue the young Indian.

"Where did the others go!" he cried, leaping to his feet.

The Indian boy rose slowly, unsheathed his long, bone-handled hunting knife, and John felt his insides tense with fear. He slipped his own knife up and, for a moment, they stood, measuring each other. John was taller, but they were about the same weight. John knew that young Indians spent hours wrestling each other, developing their strength and skill in one-on-one combat.

The Indian crouched and flashed his blade.

"I'm no Indian hater," John pleaded. "There's no need for this. I'm not like those two."

"Four," the Indian boy corrected again, feinting with the blade and testing John's reactions.

Three rifle shots boomed across the sage. John's blood froze in his veins and a line of the forgotten conversation came back to him. *Might even kill the man and use his woman!* "Oh, no!" he cried in a strangled voice. "They must be at the ranch. That woman ... they were talking about my mother!"

As he ran, a thousand demons tormented him. Why hadn't he understood the danger at once? And why, today of all days, had he chosen to hike to the spring pond and soak up its coolness instead of staying home where he was needed?

A shot, then a moment of silence, then a volley of gunfire echoed across the land. "Hang on pa, ma! Hang on! I'm coming!" he cried.

The chaparral cut at his face as he charged through it in a direct line across the mesa. His lungs burned for more air as his long, slender legs pumped until they started to cramp.

There at last was the cliff's edge and below, a mile beyond, was their cabin. Maybe there was time. But he didn't know what he could do. He'd left his old .50 caliber Hawken Rifle beside the water, but it was so heavy he'd never have been able to cover the distance at a run. He staggered to the cliff's edge and gazed out at the distant cabin he called home.

Gunsmoke hung thick in the yard, and John could see two men dodging through the brush and firing at the house. They moved in like stalking wolves, while the other two ran toward the small corral and the Reid horses.

John yelled, a high chilling call that floated down

toward the house. He saw the four twist around in his direction. As John broke into a tortured run down the steep cliff trail, he saw a flash of fire, then black smoke funneling off a torch.

Jonathan Reid burst through the doorway, firing from the hip with his Navy Colt pistol. The boy froze against the cliffside, unable to move as he stared at the man he worshipped. John's father was a big man, bull strong and a veteran fighter. As he rushed through that cabin door, with the pistol snapping out lead, four guns zeroed in on him and he took only a half dozen steps before the bullets started to rip and drain away his life's blood. The Navy Colt fell into the dirt, and his massive body pitched forward and lay still.

John's mother screamed and ran out of the cabin toward the man she loved. There were twenty years of good times and bad wrapped up in him and no tomorrows. She threw herself at his body, and a rifle's bullet slammed her sideways across the yard.

John didn't remember coming down from the cliff, screaming his anguish as he helplessly watched the outlaws rope his family's tiny band of horses and gallop away.

He reached the yard and collapsed beside his father and mother. He cried until there was nothing left inside and until those he held grew cool with the evening breeze.

He washed them and shaved pa, too, like he'd once seen the womenfolk do for those who'd departed from this world for the next. John wished he could have his mother's wedding dress from under the bed and the ironed white shirt that his father wore on special occasions. But the cabin was burnt to the ground. Nothing was left but smoldering ashes and the char-covered outline of his mother's iron stove, the pride of her home.

John smoothed the fabric on her sleeve and sat

rocking with pain, trying desperately hard to be a man and do what was right and proper. He knew that meant digging a pair of graves. He forced himself to stand and then moved over to the corral where he found the pair of shovels he and his father had often used together.

He dug for hours, and the rough covering of his palms chapped, blistered, and bled into the weathered wooden handle. With each shovelful of Texas earth, he remembered an incident, a moment he'd shared with those who lay ready for burying.

His father always boasted that his wife was the prettiest girl in west Texas. And his mother would laugh from deep inside and all of the worry would melt from her face. Then the boy could see a girlish quality in his mother that belied the harsh reality of living in Texas, in that raw and lawless land.

The Indian watched, sitting quietly only a couple of feet away. He rose to his feet and stepped over to the grave. He reached for the white boy's bloody hand and pulled it away from the handle of the shovel.

John raised his head and followed the Indian's gaze toward the gap in the hills through which the outlaws had ridden. Something passed across his eyes. A pain, a remembering of his own. It was so fleeting and subtle, nothing more than a fractional tightening of skin—yet it said everything. "I am Tonto!" he said. He took John's shovel and started digging.

Chapter 2

It was long past dark when they pitched in the final spade of earth. John stood beside the fresh mounds and tried to remember something out of the Bible that his parents would favor being spoken over them.

He couldn't dredge up anything. Not a word, even though his ma had read from the Good Book every night of his remembering life.

"Are you going to talk to the Great Spirit?" Tonto asked, after a long stillness.

"I'm tryin'," John whispered, "but the words won't come."

"It is not spoken words that the Great Spirit listens for. It is the unspoken words from your heart."

John glanced up. He could barely see Tonto in the starlight, but the young Indian's wisdom reached out soothingly, trying to help him understand.

"I loved them. It wasn't their time to die."

The Indian boy looked down at his feet. "Five winters ago, a great sickness swept through our village.

13

Many died. My mother and father and two brothers. It was like a knife that ripped out my heart."

Tonto's chin lifted to form a strong silhouette in the moonlight. "It was not *their* time, either."

John felt a rush of shame. "I, at least, have a brother. He's a Texas Ranger. Do you have . . . ?"

His words trailed off as Tonto shook his head.

"Will you carve the crosses?" the Indian asked.

He looked up quickly. "How do you know of such things?"

Tonto stiffened. "Do we not have eyes to see your burial places? Besides," he said, the roughness leaving his voice, "at the time of the great sickness, a man in black robes wearing sandals and the golden cross walked into our villages. He spoke of your Great Spirit and performed his ceremonies. My people still died. Our Medicine Man put a curse on him and he went away."

"Yes, I will carve the crosses."

Tonto nodded. "Carve them both yourself. I will do something of worth. I will cover the graves with rocks so that the wolves do not dig them up and chew their bones."

John watched Tonto as he began to gather rocks. "Why are you helping me, Tonto? Up on the mesa, you wanted to slit my throat."

"Yes. But in this place I feel your pain and know it as my own. I acted in anger while you saved my life."

In the cool sweetness of the Texas sunrise, they were still working. And, before the red ball to the east had risen above the distant rocky mesas, they were finished. For a moment, John Reid knelt beside the fresh graves, his strong calloused hands sifting the rocky soil.

Tonto swung onto his pony, stretched out an arm. "Come, John Reid."

"Where?"

"To my tribe."

"But I've got to find my brother."

"You will. In time. Come!"

He nodded, took the arm, and swung onto the pony's back. Together, they rode to the west, with the blood sky washing over their backs and the taste of ashes and destruction seeping out into the land.

They moved slowly and carefully. John thought about his brother Dan, all he had left of his family. He was only nineteen but already a veteran fighter. It was a proud thing to be a Texas Ranger. Even though many still complained about the open lawlessness of Comanche scalpers, Mexican cattle rustlers, and white horse thieves, along the Rio Grande and even far into the Panhandle country, the Rangers were making their mark. He'd find Dan and join the Texas Rangers. He'd track down the killers of his parents. Hunt them down, no matter how many years it took or how far he had to travel.

"I swear I'll kill them, Tonto!" he blurted in anger. "Texas. Mexico. New Mexico. I don't care. I'll find them or die trying."

The Indian nodded. "Without a gun or horse? You would die at their hands or at those of my enemies, the Kiowa and Comanche to the north, with their great horses, or the stealthy Apache to the west who move as one with the land and strike without being seen."

"I've heard of them," John said hotly, "and I'm not afraid. Besides, those outlaws were heading for Mexico."

"So," Tonto said, "you would walk unarmed into the wastelands of the hated Chiricahua and Mescalero? Even your Texas Rangers have not been able to subdue those peoples. What could you hope to find except slow death?"

"I've got to do something!"

"Wait. Stay with us until you are ready. I will teach you how to live and fight like one of the People. Many,

many years before my time, we came a great distance to this country. And we fought until our enemies respected our arrows and spears. Today, we live in peace with all. But it will not last."

"Why?"

"The other tribes are gathering against the white man's soldiers. Our tribe has kept the peace until now and lived by its treaty. Yet, this cannot always be, for enemies surround us on all sides. White man and red man both call us traitors."

John nodded. He could feel the despair in his young companion. It had happened before, this annihilation of the Indian people. Sometimes, whole tribes vanished as disease or enemies decimated them, like sick prairie animals. If a tribe began to weaken, they might make peace with a neighbor or agree to give up their horses or women in order to join an ally. But this was rare, for the stronger tribe never needed them and preferred to take over new territory.

"Will . . ." he paused, not wanting to sound scared but needing to know. "Will your people let me stay?"

"Perhaps," Tonto said stoically. "I will tell our council you are my friend, that you saved my life."

"Will that shame you?"

He laughed for the first time, a good boyish sound, and it seemed strange coming from his lips. "No. It will convince the elders that, instead of this good pony, I need a man's horse."

It took them three days to reach Tonto's village and, in spite of his enormous grief, John found himself enjoying Tonto's quiet companionship. The young Indian was wise in the ways of the land. He could identify every living thing and locate waterholes that a thirsty white man would pass by within fifty yards. Each evening, the young warrior set looped rawhide nooses in the brush and each day they had rabbit to eat. The Indian boy demonstrated how his short bow was capable of killing small game.

When they crested a ridge late on the third day, Tonto pointed down into a long, green valley. John's pulse quickened at the sight of a hundred colorfully painted teepees. All the teepees faced east where a large band of horses was being tended by young boys.

The women were hanging strips of buffalo meat over thickly smoking fires. Hungry dogs stood about, hoping a piece might be thrown in their direction. Small groups of women were scraping animal hides that were pegged to the ground. Working on the exposed side, the squaws removed the meat and fat with quick slashing motions of their fleshers and stone scrapers.

"So many hides!" John exclaimed.

"Yes. The buffalo gives us all we need." He pointed to the women. "Those squaws will mix the brains, liver and fat to tan the skins and then smoke them over the fires to make them watertight. The meat you see drying will be saved for winter, the horns will be used for flasks, the bones for knives, scrapers, sewing awls, and what you call ladles. Even the hooves are used as a paste for ornamental dressings."

Like most whites, John never thought much about using the buffalo for more than its choicest cuts of meat. As they drew nearer, a large pack of dogs charged towards them. They looked mean, but as soon as they were close, they began yapping excitedly as Tonto called out the names of some of his favorites.

There were only about a hundred teepees, and John realized that Tonto's tribe was not a large force, certainly not big enough to stand up to an attack from its warring neighbors.

As if reading his mind, Tonto said, "We are small, but respected for our bravery."

John never felt more alone in his life than when Tonto reined his pony to a halt and dismounted, then walked away, leaving him to face the silent stares.

John tried to smile but their eyes seemed to bore

through him. He squirmed uneasily and watched a large mongrel sniff his dangling foot. The dog's growling grew louder and when John saw its lips draw back from its teeth, he knew it was going to sink its fangs.

He kicked it and the big dog yelped and retreated. For a moment, not a sound was heard; then they began to chatter, and he saw several men laugh quietly as they smiled at him. For some reason, John relaxed and then slipped to the ground to stand waiting.

It seemed like hours that they stood there. He sat in the center of the crowd, and all the tribe gathered about him as if he were some kind of oddity. And maybe he was. In fact, the longer he waited, the worse he felt. These weren't his people. He didn't belong here.

"I can read your face clearly, John Reid. I see the pain in your eyes from the death of your mother and father." The voice was deep and soft.

The man stepped forward from out of the crowd. There was something about this man's gaze that seemed to be stripping away all the fortifications John had built up to keep the others from seeing how he felt.

"Did my eyes deceive me?"

"No, sir," he whispered tightly.

The chief moved a half step closer. "Listen well, white boy. Though we cannot see those who are dear to us even in death, they're with us always!"

John swallowed hard and leaned forward as the chief continued. "Know this," he said, with unfailing conviction thickening his voice. "Keep the memory of your mother and father close within you and they will *never* die."

"I . . . I will, sir," he said huskily. "I'll never forget them and won't rest until their killers are all dead. And I'll find them. I swear I will, if you'll loan me a horse and a spear."

Something kindled in the chief's eyes and a trace of reserve was lain aside as his big hand came out and rested on John's shoulder. "Someday, these things will be freely given as you ask. For now, you are our friend who has saved Tonto. You will stay."

"But . . ."

The chief's fingers tightened on his shoulder not hard, but with great firmness. "While you stay, do not stand apart from the People and fester inside like a deep lance wound. If you seek vengeance, you must learn the Indian ways of war and cunning or you will die, as Tonto says. We will all teach you. This is our gift in return for Tonto's life. Learn well. Become one with us."

John felt a renewal of hope, a sense that he was about to be given something that would help him carry through with his deadly resolve.

He gazed straight into the great chief's eyes and nodded stiffly. "I thank you. I will do as you say."

"Good. You have proven yourself wise as well as brave, John Reid." When he spoke, his voice was strong and absolute. "This John Reid shall become one of our People from this day always. Teach him our ways. Be his friend. Help him mend that which festers deep in his heart. Do this, I say."

The chief turned, and the tribe separated to let him pass.

John was stripped to a loincloth and mounted on a horse. The signal was given and the two lines of horsemen charged each other, hollering and shouting. He dug his heels into the mare's ribs and she leaped forward toward his opponent. This was the game called horse-throwing.

His adversary was older and a superior rider. His name was Running Elk and he'd unhorsed John many times. John's mare yielded to the pressure of his knees, and Running Elk grinned as their mounts collided. The Indian kicked and his foot caught John under the knee and lifted him. John twisted completely around on his mount and slammed an elbow into Running Elk's jaw. The Indian flew to the ground and was out of the game.

John beamed and rode in Tonto's direction, shouting, "I've beaten Running Elk. Look out, my friend, you are next."

Tonto wheeled to meet the challenge. Their horses raced past and both young men aimed hard punches at each other and scored. Twenty yards apart, they turned and charged once more. John raised himself up, feeling the blood pounding in his veins. Never had he unseated Tonto! But today, with his new trick, he *knew* he could. Tonto's horse reared and John grabbed for the Indian's leg. His friend was a better rider and proved it by throwing his weight sideways and almost dragging John to the ground. Their arms locked and they grappled, aware that their teammates were shouting them on. Then John slammed a forearm under Tonto's throat flipping him over backward.

Instantly, he was off his horse and down beside his friend. "Are you all right?"

Tonto wiped a trickle of blood from his nose and smiled grimly. "Now we try a different game."

Five minutes later, the two of them were charging toward a line of spears stuck in the ground. John could not hope to win, but he was going to try. When he came to the first spear, John bent low and yanked it free. In the same motion he buried the one he held where the first one had been. It was the supreme test of horsemanship and speed. A favorite game of skill.

A shout of appreciation went up as he exchanged two more spears just as smoothly. He smiled with growing confidence, when he realized he was ahead of Tonto by two horse strides. One more spear, he thought, and I've beaten him at last!

It was his downfall. John managed to yank the spear free but, as he tried to plant its exchange, he leaned out too far and fell, very nearly impaling himself on the shaft and knocking the wind from his chest. He lay gasping like a beached fish.

Tonto streaked by, neatly exchanging spears and his team convulsed with laughter at the white boy who lay doubled up on the ground. Tonto wheeled his horse and galloped back to dismount.

"Now it's my turn. Are *you* all right?" The turn-about made them all laugh except John—but he wasn't angry—just frustrated that he still hadn't sur-passed his skilled friend.

Days stretched into weeks and the games continued, as did his education in the arts of fighting with a club, a spear and, especially, a knife. The training was hard and it seemed at times that every man and boy in camp went out of his way to deliver knocks in the guise of experience. Each day, he awoke so stiff and sore he could barely move; yet, each night as he fell asleep under the silvery blanket of stars, he felt tougher—stronger—quicker—than he'd ever believed possible.

At first, he'd not been able to wrestle with those his own age. True, he was stronger than most of them, but they were so fast! Before he quite realized what was happening, one of them would be flipping him into the dirt while the ring of onlookers roared with delight.

Not today, he vowed as he entered the ring. He moved in slowly, trying hard to guess what Tonto would do and knowing he couldn't. The young Indian never repeated his moves in the same order. He dove for John's leg, catching it up and lifting him off the ground. As Tonto strained for balance, John man-aged to get an armlock around his opponent's neck and they crashed onto the body-churned earth. John came up first, but Tonto dove and caught him below the knees. They seemed perfectly matched; today it could go either way.

Tonto, his body wet as an eel, slipped behind John, who reached down and grabbed his friend's ankle, straining to pull it up until the blood vessels in his strong arms stood out like bow-strings.

"John!" came the cry. "Johnny!"

21

He ripped Tonto's leg up and slammed him to the earth, then barreled through the stunned onlookers. "Dan!" he shouted happily, throwing himself into his brother's arms. "I *knew* you'd find me."

Dan blinked away tears. He was a handsome man, only nineteen but full-bodied and tall. "Goddamn, it's good to see you, little brother. I'd have come sooner but we were on ranger business down in Mexico when it all happened."

"Did you go after them?" he asked, bitterness flooding back with a rush.

Dan looked away. "We took up tracks. Damn near rode our horses to death chasing them down into Mexico."

His lips tightened and a hard line came to his young mouth. "John, there was four, right?"

He nodded, holding his breath.

"And they were leading that bay horse that toed out on the right front."

"Yeah."

"Comancheros got 'em. They paid for what they did."

"Are you sure?" He *had* to know. There could be no mistakes about this.

"Pretty sure, John. Pretty damn sure. I'll guarantee they died hard and bad." He spat tobacco juice at the earth. "That make you feel any better?"

John turned away. His eyes met Tonto's and he said, "Yeah, Dan, I guess maybe it does."

"Chief," Dan said, "I'm going to make a report of how you took in my brother. You have no reason to love the whites."

"A child has no color."

"Thank you, chief. I won't ever forget this. And, someday, maybe what I have to say about you and your people will count," Dan said, taking John's arm and walking off to speak with him in private.

It was late afternoon when the young Texas Ranger

finally told John the thing that so deeply troubled his mind.

"I ain't going to argue with you, John, and you're too big to try and whip, so I'm asking you to just trust me and do as I say."

John couldn't imagine why his brother was so troubled now that they were finally reunited. Everything was going to be fine now, why . . .

"John, I'm sending you away. Back east to mother's sister in Detroit."

"But, why!" he shouted, jumping to his feet. "I don't want to go back there. I belong in Texas!"

"You've got to, boy. Ma and Pa always dreamed of you going east to get an education."

"Then why didn't *you* go!" he wailed. "You're the oldest."

"Because . . . well, because I just didn't, that's all. And I don't want you growing up to be like me."

"Why not? Dan, I don't understand you. Being a Texas Ranger is . . ."

"Long hours, low pay, and not too many years of livin'." He shook his head stubbornly. "Nope. I live by the gun and one of these days I'll die by one and nothing much will have changed for my having been on this earth. But with you . . . well, it's going to be different. You're going to be someone important and the only way that happens is by books."

"Dan, *please*. I never disobeyed Pa and I'd do anything to see that things come out like they wanted, but . . ."

"No," Dan choked, "you gotta go. Don't you see why? And . . . and, after you get that education, you can always come back."

John bit his lip until the tears stung his eyes. Then, slowly, he turned away to locate his friend and tell him good-bye, and that he was leaving Texas—that it would be years before he could fulfill the wish of his dead parents.

But first, he looked at his brother. "I'll do it," he

rasped, "because of them and because of you. But then I'm coming back. I swear I will!"

His brother nodded with a single jerk of his chin. "Thank you, John. Thank you."

They stood beside their horses as the morning sun bathed the land with a soft golden color. The chief stepped up, bid farewell to the young Texas Ranger, and then turned to John.

"You will be a wise hunter, for you have learned well and your heart is brave and good. You will become a great man among your people."

John's chin quivered. He was filled with gratitude toward the chief and these people. He desperately wanted to tell this great warrior how he felt.

"You have taken me into your village as one of your own and have taught me your secrets. That we are brothers until death and that the white man and the red can live and grow with one another. No matter how far I go from this place, you and Tonto and the members of your tribe will be in my heart forever. And I promise, mighty chief, that I will always live my life so you may call me brother and be proud!"

He took a ragged breath and turned to face Tonto. They looked deep into each other's eyes. John took out his hunting knife and with his eyes never leaving Tonto's face, he drew the blade across the palm of his right hand. The warm blood oozed forth and dripped down to the earth at his feet.

Tonto took John's knife and cut his own palm. The only pain they felt was in their hearts.

They clasped hands, squeezing as tight as they could until their blood mixed and flowed between them. Tonto finally released his grip and removed the great turquoise and silver amulet that had been his father's and his grandfather's before. He tied it around John's neck.

The young Indian was a warrior and did not wish to

show his emotions before the watchful gaze of his people. His black eyes were misted and in a husky voice he said, "From this moment, wherever you go, whatever you do, you will always be Kemo Sabe."

They clasped hands again and Tonto whispered, "Kemo Sabe—Trusted Friend!"

Chapter 3

THE Wells Fargo stage crawled across the vast country, dwarfed by the towering red buttes, golden mesas with deep blue canyons, and the sun-blasted valley floor. Even the soaring eagles flew no higher than the huge sculpted sandstone sentinels.

The handsome young attorney gazed out the coach window and drank in the beauty. His brown eyes missed nothing of the vistas he'd been dreaming about these past fourteen years. He'd done exceptionally well at law school and had received numerous offers of employment in the east. But this was home and he knew he had to return.

"Say, young fella, you sure you don't want to play a hand or two of stud poker?"

John Reid shook his head at his fellow traveler, Mr. Nash, a professional gambler. He turned back toward the window.

"Dammit, this is the most unsporting group of men I've ever had the misfortune to be penned up with," Nash grumbled.

"Perhaps," John suggested, "we'll pick up someone more to your liking at the next relay station. The driver said there's often a passenger or two waiting."

"I sure as hell hope so," Nash crabbed as he shuffled and reshuffled a worn deck of cards. "I mean— hellfire! I could understand it if you three were down-and-out cowpokes, but I got a hunch you all got more money than I do."

The heavyset German shook his jowls disapprovingly. "You vood like to change that, ya?"

Nash grinned. "Sure as it's day, Mr. Weiner. I make no apologies for my intentions or profession."

The German looked away, his small, deep-set eyes glittered with disapproval.

"Say, Mister Lee. I've heard you Chinamen like to gamble. How about it?"

Mr. Lee, who might have been thirty or fifty, slowly turned and smiled before saying, in precise English, "No thank you, sir. My limited funds serve only to carry me to my family in San Francisco."

"Well—horseshit!" swore the angry gambler. "I sure am eager for some fresh company. It's been more than a week since I've felt the stirring of blood that comes only from high-stakes poker."

John Reid smiled. He knew Nash's kind. There'd even been some of them in college. They'd used the same weary technique of insulting one's honor as a sporting man. It seldom failed.

"Mr. Nash. You won't have long to wait. There's the next station."

Through the dust in the waystation yard, John saw that this place was just like all the others. It was made of crumbling adobe with a sod roof and a stove pipe chimney sticking out on top. An old dog slumbered by the front door, and its hairless tail slapped at flies. A huge mound of rusty cans was piled against the eastern wall, and John counted six wrecked Concord stages out back. They'd been cannibalized for extra parts, and the wheels on all but one were gone; they lay on their sides like busted beetles. A small, sagging corral completed the scene.

As they drew up to the yard, a Mexican with worn saddle bags thrown across his shoulder came out of the station door and flashed his brilliant white teeth.

"Aiee, amigos!"

Behind him, an Indian woman was carrying a monogrammed valise. She placed it beside her grinning husband and moved toward the water trough.

The Mexican twisted around to the doorway, cupped his hands around his mouth, and yelled, "Senorita! They are here."

A young woman hurried out into the bright sunlight, her hair glistening like morning dew on a grainfield. John Reid blinked and stared out his window with open appreciation. In a flash, he disembarked and moved in her direction.

"Afternoon, ma'am!"

She glanced at him coolly. "Driver?" she called, looking up on the coach.

The young man riding shotgun gazed down at her. Whatever this girl needed, he figured to supply. "Yes, ma'am?"

"Would you mind putting this valise up top and making certain it's secured properly?"

"Yes, ma'am! I'll do it myself."

John couldn't help but grin. Up to now, his observation had been that the shotgun guard either thought himself too important to speak with a lowly passenger, or else he was a mute.

John strolled around the yard, his eyes never going far from the girl. Pretty, too pretty for this country, but cold as ice, he decided, kicking a bean can fifteen yards across the sage.

It was a fast stage stop, just long enough for the Indian woman to water the team and for the old driver to check the traces, take a fast swallow from a goatskin

31

bag, and then holler for everyone to get the hell on board. He was pulling out.

The girl hesitated. "This stage *is* going to Del Rio, isn't it, driver?"

"Sure is, ma'am," the young guard offered, "and . . ."

"Shet up, Charley!" the driver snapped. *"I'm* the goddam driver. Not you. Del Rio, huh? Yeah, young lady. We're going to Del Rio. Now, are you?"

"Of course."

"Then get on board!" he shouted.

John saw the deep blush of embarrassment color the girl's face. Maybe she wasn't so unfeeling, he thought.

The Mexican, with great dash and chivalry, bowed and opened the door. John leaned out of his seat and offered the lady his hand.

"May I help you up?"

She almost accepted, but not quite. "Thank you," she said, hauling herself inside, "but I can manage."

As she stood trying to decide where she could possibly sit, the Mexican slammed the door behind her. A whip cracked like a shot and the coach catapulted forward.

The girl pitched over sideways—right into John's waiting arms. It was an accident, but one that he could not have planned any better. She sprawled across his lap, soft and sweet-smelling and fighting like a Comanche to pull her dress down and preserve some dignity.

It was too late. John's lips were only inches from hers and, in his mildest tone, he said, "You were absolutely right, ma'am, you managed it *very* well."

Her face went crimson. Her mouth opened to speak but she couldn't find the words to express her outrage.

"Holy cow!" Nash swore. "Look at the money she's got!"

The entire floor of the coach was layered with money

that had poured out of the valise she'd dropped. The girl fell to her knees and frantically tried to scoop up the cash and stuff it back inside the bag.

The pudgy German, who'd been so nervous about raiding Indians and highwaymen, chose that moment to try a joke. "Vell," he proclaimed, "she don't look like a vestern bad man."

No one laughed. The Chinaman seemed very ill at ease and averted his eyes. Nash, the gambler, beamed down at the money so hugely that his face seemed to split across the middle.

"Young lady, I just bet you've always wanted to learn how to play poker."

She glared at him. "You are wrong."

"May I help you?" John asked, leaning forward to pick up some of the bills.

"Don't touch them!"

He drew back. "I wouldn't dream of it, ma'am. But if we're going to be so cramped, allow me to make the introductions. We might as well try and make the best of things."

Her name was Amy Striker and, once she had her money tucked away, and her dress pushed back down below her pretty ankles, her disposition improved markedly. It was clear to all, however, that she preferred to be left to her reading.

But something seemed to bother her and John couldn't quite put his finger on it until she set her book down with exasperation and said, "Would one of you gentlemen across from me mind trading places? I just can't seem to read traveling backwards."

Nash, who was still miffed at her initial rebuke, made no attempt at niceties. "Lady, I'm staying put. You don't wanna play poker—I don't wanna move."

"Very well," she said tightly, looking at John.

What the heck, he thought. "All right."

As they changed seats, their hands brushed and it was something John figured he liked just fine.

"That was kind of you, Mister Reid," Amy said, taking her place.

"Thank you, ma'am. I hope you can read now."

She actually smiled. And it was like a candle illuminating a cave. Warm. Glowing.

"I'm sure I can, now," she chimed sweetly as she opened her book.

It was by Helen Hunt Jackson, one of his favorite authors. "She's quite good, isn't she?"

The girl seemed genuinely surprised. "You would know?"

"Yes. But actually I preferred her *Century of Dishonor.*"

"Really? I've been dying to read it, but I cannot seem to get a copy."

"Keep trying," he advised seriously. "It's well worth the effort."

She nodded, and looked at him pensively before returning to her book. "Thank you, Mister Reid. I shall."

"But, Miss Striker?"

"Yes?"

"You're really missing it."

"What?"

"That," John said, pointing out at the sentinel mesas, the sweeping majesty of the earth around them.

"Oh." She nodded politely. "I'm afraid I've seen quite enough of it these past twelve days."

"Where did you come from?"

"Civilization, Mister Reid. Civilization."

Her eyes dropped back to the pages and, though he knew his interruption would probably annoy her, he wanted to talk with this girl. About the book, its author, where she was going—anything!

But first—he needed an opening. Staring with unseeing eyes at the buttes, he came up with what he hoped would be passable and smiled warmly. "Kind of funny, isn't it, ma'am?"

A shadow of irritation crossed her lovely face and seemed to make her eyes bluer. "What is?"

He wished he'd kept quiet, but it was too late now. "Well," he stammered, "the fact that you like to *read* and my name is *Reid*. Get it? We have a lot in common."

She stared at him in amazement.

"I guess you don't. Never mind," he said, lamely.

Later that afternoon, as the sun plunged lower against the horizon, it glowed with bright intensity into the coach, causing them all to squint. Especially John, who was peering out to the west.

"Young man," Weiner said gently, "Please excuse me. But the sun. It is too bright. You will ruin your eyes."

John shielded his face from the glare.

"Ya, I mean it," the German continued. "It vill burn the retina. Bad. Very bad."

He poked his broad chest with pride. "I know. I am an optometrist from Dusseldorf."

"What are you doing out here?"

"I show you," Weiner said, reaching inside his jacket, aware that he'd suddenly become the focus of everyone's attention. His chubby little hand produced a pair of eyeglasses with strange, dark lenses.

"What are these?"

He winked conspiratorially. "My invention. They are *solar spectacles!* And I have come to the vest to market them. Vit all dis sun I get rich, ya?"

John nodded and saw that Amy was watching his reaction closely. Nash grunted in open derision.

"You just might have something, Mr. Weiner," John said, trying to wipe the contempt off the gambler's face. "Mind if I try them?"

"Sure. Go on. Then tell me vot you tink."

John placed them over his nose, hooked the wire frames over each ear and blinked owlishly. "I can't see anything."

"Ya!" Weiner said proudly. "Dey really vork!"

"How do I look?"

"Much better," Amy giggled. "A definite improvement."

"Thanks, ma'am. When I set up my law practice, I'll wear them to court so I can't see the judge's face. That way I won't be able to tell whether I am winning my case or not. Suspense, you know."

He handed the eyeglasses back to Weiner. "I think you'll be able to sell a pair to every man, woman, and child in Texas."

"Ya, I vill for sure! Vork hard. Send money to my vife and children in Dusseldorf. Dey vant to be cowboys and Indians, you know. In America, you can be anyting. *Dat's* opportunity!"

Several moments later, Amy looked at John. "Where do you intend to practice law, Mr. Reid?"

John pretended to give the question a great deal of consideration although, actually, he allowed it none at all. He was counting on Dan's advice. "Where did you say you were going to, ma'am?"

"Del Rio. But . . ."

"You know, I *like* the sound of that place. Bet it's just waiting for an eager young attorney. Maybe you'd be good enough to show me around when we get there."

She looked him square in the eyes. Her lips parted with amusement. "Maybe I will," she said lightly.

"Good! And if . . ."

His words were cut off by the sound of a gunshot and a cry from the guard above. A chunk of wood ripped off the coach. In the same instant, there was a deafening blast from Charlie's shotgun.

"Vot is wrong?" Weiner cried.

John peered out the window, then ducked back inside. "Ma'am," he said quietly, "I think you'd better get down on the floor again and hide that bag of loot. It seems we're under attack."

The German paled. The Chinaman sat like a statue,

and the gambler nervously spilled his cards all over his lap.

Amy Striker's face grew resolute. "Can we outrun them? Hold them off?"

John ducked his head outside for an instant and almost took a bullet in the brain for his trouble.

"Ma'am," he said quietly, "you'd best do as I say. I don't think we're going to outshoot *or* outrun them."

Amy nodded and hit the floor.

Chapter 4

JOHN could hear the driver yelling at the young shotgun. "Aim for their horses!" The guard clearly was no rifleman. In fact, he hadn't scored once against the four outlaws who were rapidly closing the distance.

"Goddammit, kid. It's their horses or our lives!"

"No!" the young guard yelled, firing and then calling, "I got one! Winged through the . . ."

John heard him grunt with pain, then saw his body pitch off the coach. But his boot caught in the top railing. He hung upside down and began to flop against the window.

Amy cried out at the boy's empty face that dangled and slapped before them.

"Stay low!" John ordered, shoving her head back toward the floor.

"What the hell is the driver doing?" the gambler shouted. "He can't outrun them!"

"He's going to try," John answered gravely.

"That's a dumb thing to do. Stupid enough to get us all killed!"

Amy's head popped up. "Don't any of you have a gun?"

The gambler swallowed, "Yeah, I do, lady."

"Then why aren't you using it!"

"I haven't any money to lose. It's not my fight."

"Vell, it's mine," Weiner thundered. "Give it to me! I am not afraid of vestern bad men. I am no coward."

"You're a fool. Here, it's just a derringer. Be my guest."

John glanced out the window. One of the outlaws was nearly parallel to them. He wore a hood and was whipping his mount furiously.

"Stay down, Mr. Weiner! Nash is right. You can't help with a derringer. Start shooting and . . ."

The German didn't listen. Maybe he'd read some of those eastern dime novels where heroes are bigger than life. In any case, he pushed his head and arm through the window and took aim. The outrider swung his gun in response and the two weapons barked simultaneously.

Weiner missed. The outlaw did not.

"Ahh!" he cried as he slammed back inside and sprawled across John. His eyelids fluttered, his lips twitched, and then he died. He was shot through the chest pocket. As John rolled him aside, Weiner's solar spectacles tumbled out; one lens was bullet blasted.

Amy was on her knees at once. "Is he . . ."

"Dead?" John nodded sadly. "Yes."

"So much for American opportunity," Nash muttered.

But even as they stared at Weiner, they could hear gunshots and knew that the driver, in his own stubborn fury, had no intention of pulling to a stop and having his stage robbed.

They all peered out the window and saw a rider go down under his horse, get pinned, yank off his hood, and cry, "Gattlin! Gattlin! My leg. Help me!"

The remaining three didn't waste so much as a glance in his direction as they thundered on in pursuit.

John's gun was in his valise in the stage boot and he cursed his own stupidity. Yet, given the circumstances, it would have been irresponsible to open fire anyway; to do so would invite the death of an innocent passenger—Weiner was proof enough of that.

"There's one on this side," John gritted. "He's going after our horses."

"Two over here," Nash answered, peeking over the door frame.

The outlaw streaked by John, and suddenly they heard the driver shout in pain and heard him thud into the well. "I've been hit!"

"Hell!" Nash cried, "that fool is going to get us all killed. We're a runaway!"

The outlaw, riding low in the saddle, finally breasted the wheel team of horses; he dropped his reins and jumped onto the nearest one's back. John was amazed at this daring. Realizing that he was in no immediate danger, he leaned far out and watched the outlaw swing down onto the traces and start jumping his way forward to the leaders. Incredibly, he reached them and began pulling them in. Then, a gunshot from the well above blasted him between the shoulders, and he arched upward and then toppled under the flying hooves. A long scream filled the air.

"We're going to crash!" the gambler wailed, "and when one of these things flips, there ain't no tomorrow for whoever is inside."

John glanced down at the girl and saw her looking directly at him as they both felt the stage begin a whipping motion.

"Do you promise to show me Del Rio?"

She blinked. Nodded up and down jerkily.

"Then see you later, ma'am." He stood up, reached outside and his fingers located the top luggage railing.

With a twist of his long body, he swung through the window. He used all of his strength to keep from being thrown under the stage and to pull himself to the top. He rolled forward and dropped into the well, snatching up the fallen reins.

"You don't have a chance!" the wounded driver hissed, between clenched teeth.

John shot a fierce look at the two outlaws galloping alongside. "We never did, mister," he replied, as he began to pull the horses in.

"Whoa up there! Whoa!"

The horses were coated with lather and nearly ready to drop from exhaustion. Even so, they were badly spooked and it took a lot of sawing on the lines to bring them to a halt.

"Outside," one of the outlaws yelled, pointing his gun through the window. His partner galloped around to the other side and glared up at John.

"You up there. Throw down the strongbox."

John searched the well. "There isn't one."

The outlaw leveled his pistol at John and cocked it.

"He's tellin' the truth, damn you!" the wounded driver raged. "All we got is a mail pouch full of letters and packages. They ain't worth getting killed for."

"Then why didn't you pull up?"

The driver settled into a guilty silence while John helped the passengers out of the coach. One out of the pair of road agents roughly upended the mail pouch and scattered its contents all over the ground.

"I told you so," the driver spat.

"The mail pouch is what we're after."

"Let's go!"

"You mean just leave 'em?"

"Them's our orders."

But the second man had other ideas. "Hell," he argued, "who's gonna know if we search the passengers? We can both use the money."

The other outlaw hesitated a moment and then weakened. "Well, maybe . . . if we make it quick."

"Hell, yes! I'll have 'em shet of their valuables in no time. Line up."

He started with the gambler. Backhanded him for not having anything of value. Then he stepped up before John. He was a rough, dirty man in grease-stained clothes and a gray hood with two eye-holes. John guessed he hadn't seen soap and water in years.

"What do you got?"

"A few dollars."

"Empty your pockets, dude. And don't try to be a hero in front of the young lady."

"I wouldn't dream of it," John said tightly, knowing that if this man noticed the treasured silver and turquoise amulet he wore under his shirt and tie, he would have to fight.

But the highwayman moved along. He shoved the Chinaman against the coach and laughed when he took more than a hundred dollars in gold jewelry from a thin, ivory-inlaid case.

"I'll check that fool laying inside. I shot him back aways."

Knocking the Chinaman aside, the man jumped into the coach.

Moments passed and John could hear him working frantically. He realized what was going on. The outlaw had discovered Amy's valise and all the money!

"What's taking you so long?" his gun-waving partner bellowed impatiently.

"I'm coming. He's a fat one, but he has a couple of dollars on him and a big gold watch. And I found the lady's bag. Nothin' worth keeping inside."

"Well, hurry it up!"

"Sure enough."

When he pushed erect in the coach, John saw at once that he was carrying about an inch of extra padding around the belly.

The bandit outside swaggered up to Amy.

"I'll check you myself, purty thing. Show me what you got."

45

"Nothing. Stay away."

"Aw, come on," he wheedled, drawing up close as she stood rigidly in line.

Out of the corner of his eye, John could see her face and knew that Amy Striker was scared, yet under control.

"Honey, you gonna produce? Or am I going to have to search you? Either way is going to be my pleasure."

John could hear her breathing faster. "I . . . don't have anything," she whispered shakily as she faltered backward against the coach.

"Sure you do!" he laughed. "And I'm going to have a good look."

His arm reached out and gripped her shoulder; he started to paw at her dress.

It was the moment John had been waiting for. He moved with the speed and precision of an Indian warrior. In a single motion, he grabbed the outlaw and wrestled him to the ground. He took a glancing blow from the man's rifle but then yanked it away as he struck the hooded face with bone-crunching punches.

The raider in the coach lifted and cocked his gun and pointed it down at John's upraised face. "All right, hero, I told you . . ." There was no way he could miss, and nothing John could do but watch him squeeze the trigger and then meet eternity rushing out of a gun-barrel.

Something flashed in the sunlight, whistled, and whirred in a silvery blur, and then John saw the knife bury itself to the hilt in the outlaw's thigh. The man screeched in agony, and his gun fell as he grabbed his leg and crashed out the doorway.

John snapped it up and whirled to see the little Chinaman straighten his coat, then march forward to retrieve his weapon. Without a trace of emotion, he yanked it out of the man's leg and wiped off the blood. He took one look, then knelt beside the outlaw who was rolling in pain and grabbed him by the hair. He drew back the man's head to reveal the exposed throat. With a trial pass, he slashed at the air, then he began the execution.

"No!" John yelled.

The Chinaman, knife poised expertly, glanced up at John. His eyes were questioning.

"Go on!" Nash ranted. "Butcher the sonovabitch!"

"No!" John repeated, picking up the fallen rifle. "It's done. The law will handle this now."

He made the outlaw put all of Amy's money back into her valise. Then, he securely roped and tied them along with the dead shotgun on the roof of the stage before asking the passengers to return inside. There was no time to waste. The driver needed medical attention at once, and the knife wound was pretty deep.

"Mr. Reid?"

He turned, about to climb up on the stage. "Yes, ma'am?"

She seemed almost shy now, a trifle embarrassed. "Well, I just . . . just wanted to say thank you."

"For what?"

"For doing all those brave things—climbing up top so we didn't turn over. Then, when that . . . that dirty beast started to touch me, you acted at great risk."

Now it was his turn to blush. "I think," he said quietly, "any gentleman would have done the same."

Her eyes brimmed with newfound admiration. "Perhaps, but I doubt it. And what I'm quite certain about is that few—very, very few—would have been successful."

He didn't know what to say, so he grabbed at the coach and prepared to climb up onto the driver's seat.

Her hand rested on his forearm and restrained him for a moment. "John? May I call you John?"

"Why certainly, Miss Striker!"

"Amy. John, I wanted to tell you something else. I'd be proud and happy to show you the town of Del Rio."

John took the lines and warned the two outlaws that any funny moves on their part would result in their being tossed off the high-rolling coach.

He slapped leather and the team vaulted into a long-striding prairie gallop. It was an exhilarating feeling! He looked at the sky, the towering buttes, and mesas and felt the wind in his face. And, beyond all that, down below was the prettiest girl in Texas who was going to show him the town where he just might hang his shingle.

Heady things! It sure was great to be back out west!

Chapter 5

DEL Rio loomed up ahead on the flat Texas plain. John had been handling the Wells Fargo team of horses like he'd done it for years, and soon he would get the wounded driver to a doctor. Then he could start hunting for his brother.

John was looking forward to telling his brother about helping to capture the pair and doing it unarmed. He'd been worrying about Dan for years. He hadn't heard from him since he'd graduated and served his duty as a Union soldier. Dan had simply stopped responding to his letters. The only feasible explanation was that the Texas Ranger had taken a secret identity and infiltrated one of the outlaw gangs along the border. That would be like Dan, to accept the riskiest assignment. But John had continued writing, hoping that someday his brother would make contact.

"Watch where you're agoin'," the driver snorted. "I sure can't keep my eye on you and these rattlesnakes at the same time!"

The horses were running dead straight on the trail. They knew feed and water, a good rubdown and some well-earned rest awaited just ahead—a man couldn't have driven them off the trail with six pairs of arms.

"You know, young fella, you ain't worth a damn right now, but you've got the hands to be a pretty fair teamster. Could be, after the Wells Fargo Company hears of your helping the stage, I could get you a job."

"Driving?"

"Course not! Shovelin' horse manure. You prove yourself, then you move up."

"I see," John replied. "Trouble is, I'm a lawyer and I'm planning to go into practice. Maybe in Del Rio."

"Lawyer!" The driver hooted in derision. "Hellfire, I'm talkin' about a *real* job, with a solid future."

"Yes, but . . ."

"Lawyers ain't good for nothin' out here 'cept drawin' up a dying man's will."

John knew it was senseless to argue, yet he couldn't help saying he thought there was plenty of need for more law.

"More law? More law! Goddamn if the law just don't get in folks' ways oftener than not. Someone shoots someone in the back, we've got a sheriff to gun the varmint down."

"What if he shoots him in the front?"

"Fair fight?" the driver asked suspiciously.

"Yes."

"He goes free. Drinks on the house!"

John shook his head. "What if it wasn't fair?"

"Judge sentences him to hang then, and we all go on a binge," the driver chortled. "Say, there, watch where you're going! Damned if I ain't gonna feel relieved to reach Del Rio. Damned if maybe I didn't make a mistake about you having a future with Wells Fargo."

John chuckled. It wasn't every day a person won and lost a promising career within five minutes, he thought, as they rolled into town.

"Hey! What happened!" a storekeeper yelled.

"Stage got hit," the driver shouted. "Tell the doc and the mortician to come arunnin'. Oh yeah, and tell your uppity sheriff, Justin A. Wiatt, to get off his officious bee-hind and come take a look."

A small boy raced up the main street yelling, "They held up the Overland Stage! They held it up and shot and killed some people!"

A handsome man wearing a printer's apron ran out of an office that bore the sign—DEL RIO REGISTER & DISPATCH—Lucas Striker, Editor. He was pale with alarm. "Driver! Is Amy Striker all right?"

John nodded. He had a sinking feeling. He should have guessed that someone as pretty as Amy would already have a man. "She's fine," he called. "Just fine."

"Thank God!"

It seemed that news traveled fast in Del Rio. By the time John hauled the coach before the stage office, a large crowd had already gathered. Some looked worried, most just acted curious, but not the beefy, red-faced man wearing the sheriff's badge.

"What the hell happened?" he bellowed.

The driver spat in the street. "What do you think? A robbery, of course! They killed our shotgun guard and a passenger. There was four of 'em."

He prodded one of the bound prisoners hard with his Winchester. "This is what's left."

Sheriff Wiatt sneered. "To make up for the two that got away, be damned if I won't see they each hang twice!"

The crowd applauded loudly.

"Did any of you get a good look at the others?"

"Hell, no! They was all wearin' the gray hoods."

The sheriff made a big display of wincing.

"You don't have to spell it out no plainer," he said angrily. "If they was hooded, it was the Cavendish gang. I received a telegram saying you'd be carryin' some land grants. Did they take 'em?"

"Nope. Probably cause they're hidden up in the boot."

"Good man!"

John saw Amy and the other two passengers move into the crowd. The girl was calling for Lucas and searching frantically for her husband. He looked around at the other faces, and his eyes scanned the town. Maybe Del Rio wasn't big enough for a law practice anyway. Only a couple of streets. One thing sure, he didn't need Amy to show him the sights.

"There ain't no use stirring up a posse," the sheriff drawled. "Them that got away will tell Butch Cavendish how robbin' stages ain't so easy these days with the law makin' its stand."

John saw Amy and the editor run into each other's arms. It wasn't such a fine day after all. "Who's Butch Cavendish?" he asked, dropping to the street.

"Mister, if you don't know, then you'll just have to ask somebody else, 'cause I ain't got time to explain the answer to such a fool question. Everyone for a hundred miles on both sides of the border knows the Cavendish gang. They been raising hell around here for years."

"Then why don't you get together a posse and arrest them?"

The sheriff stared at him as if he was crazy. "Arrest 'em! What do you think I got here?"

"I don't know," John said flatly. He was beginning to be irritated with this blustery loudmouth and was growing more and more certain that he didn't want to open a practice in a town stupid enough to elect this kind of man.

"Well, I'll tell you. I got two underpaid, overworked deputies and Butch Cavendish has a goddamn army! Even the Texas Rangers have backed off his trail."

"I don't believe that."

Sheriff Wiatt was about to explode. John could see it in the way his meaty face turned dark and brooding. The young lawyer cut him off by asking one of the deputies a question. "What's going to happen to those two outlaws?"

"We'll haul 'em over to the county seat in San Antone."

"Do you need a deposition?"

"You got one you want to get rid of?"

"Never mind," John said, moving away in disgust.

"Mister Reid? Oh, Mister Reid!"

John turned to see the editor hurrying toward him with Amy holding his arm.

"My name is Lucas Striker," he said extending an ink-stained hand.

John looked at Amy and wanted to leave. "Glad to meet you, Mister Striker."

"Likewise, sir. Amy told me what you did out there and I can't thank you enough. Why, if anything had happened to her, I'd . . ."

"Your wife showed a lot of courage, Mister Striker."

Striker glanced at Amy, then the two of them burst out laughing.

"John," she said, "I'm not his wife. I'm his niece."

Amy giggled and squeezed his hand warmly. "Can you have supper with us very soon?"

"Yes, ma'am! Right after I find the nearest Texas Ranger office."

"Are you joining?"

"No. My brother is . . ."

"Captain Dan Reid!" The editor exclaimed, snapping his fingers. "Of course! I'm surprised I didn't catch the resemblance at once. Why, you're even taller than Dan."

"*Captain* Reid?" John cried. "You mean he's a captain now?"

"You bet. He's one of the finest men ever to take the oath and badge. Dan's a hero in these parts."

His brother was alive! And famous! A captain! He could hardly wait to see him again.

"Where is he?"

Lucas Striker smiled and pointed toward the opposite end of town. "The ranger compound is at the end of the street. Can't miss it with its big American flag waving. Headquarters is right next to the bunkhouse and corrals. Big adobe structure. That's Captain Reid's office."

John snatched the editor's hand and pumped it gratefully. He impulsively grabbed Amy Striker and lifted her off the ground and swung her in a full circle before setting her down.

"Captain Reid! Wahoo!" he yelled, breaking into a run. "I'll see you later. Don't forget your promise to show me the town."

"By the time you get to the ranger compound, you've seen it," Amy yelled. "But I'd love to show it to you all over again."

John sprinted almost all the way. He counted two law offices, but that didn't matter. Not now. The American flag crackled in the northeast breeze as he raced by a sentry and burst inside.

"Dan! Dan!"

And old man laid his newspaper aside. "What do you want?" he asked suspiciously.

"To see my brother, Dan Reid."

His guarded look vanished and the man resumed his reading. "Your brother and the men are out on patrol. They might not even get back today."

John's face fell. He took a deep breath and expelled it slowly. "Oh. But . . . but then again they could ride in any time, couldn't they?"

"Sure, but I don't think you want to wait."

"Watch me," Dan said flatly. "I've been waiting fourteen years to see my brother again and I'm not budging until I do."

"Suit yourself, young fella. You can hole up in the captain's office until he arrives. Tonight. Tomorrow. Next week or next month."

"I'll still be waiting."

The man shrugged, his eyes raked the fine suit John

wore. "You don't favor your big brother much, do you?"

John awoke to the sound of muffled hoofbeats coming slowly into the compound and then the creaking of leather as the riders dismounted. Outside, it was early morning, but already the sun was hot. He rose from the couch and pushed his feet into his boots. He barreled out of the office and halted in midstride when he saw his brother. For a moment all he could think of was how much older Dan appeared, much older than he should. He looked like he hadn't slept for days.

"Dan," he whispered. "Dan!"

John ran toward him, ignoring the startled look on his brother's face.

"Dan! I can't believe it's all past now. That we're together again. Look at you! A captain!"

Dan pushed him away.

Something was *very* wrong. "What's the matter! Didn't you get any of my letters?"

"Yes," he answered slowly, "I got 'em."

John rubbed his face, the joy inside withering under his brother's hard stare. "I . . . don't understand," he whispered. "If you got them, why didn't you write back?"

Dan turned and walked stiffly away. His voice was like a whip. "You and I have nothing left in common."

"Nothing in common! I'm your brother. Remember me? This is John Reid. Your only brother!"

Dan whirled. "You're a Texas traitor! No brother of mine would bear arms against the Confederacy!"

Now he understood. Saw everything in the naked light of truth. Traitor. The Confederacy. That terrible, terrible war.

He took a deep breath. "You told me to go away and become a man. You *sent* me away though I begged to remain. And then, when I reached manhood, I had to choose between the north and the south. Only that wasn't really it at all, Captain Reid."

"The hell . . ."

"Let me finish!" John raged. "I've always listened to you. It's my turn now. The *real* issue was whether or not one man—any man—could own another. Like a dog or a horse, only sometimes not even with that much respect."

"They're slaves."

"People!" John shouted. "They are *people*. With all the same needs and hopes and feelings you and I have inside. And . . . and so I believed enough to fight when Mister Lincoln told us all men are created equal. I did what I believed in, just as pa always taught us. Dan, the war broke people, tore them up, inside and out, and then hurled them into a garbage pile and left 'em good for nothing and no one. It's over. Bury it and don't let it kill how we feel about each other. *Don't* let it do that to us now!"

Dan's strong face began to twitch and his mouth worked silently as a terrible struggle raged inside. The tears boiled up in his eyes as he shut them tightly and reached out, "Johnny! Oh, Johnny, you're all I've got left in the world!"

It was late evening and they sat beside the fire and ended their stories. It was the older brother who talked and talked, as though speaking of his battles and his loneliness would help him make sense of his life. The enormous amount of whiskey he consumed helped to loosen his tongue.

"This is Linda," he said bitterly, hauling out a picture. "And the boy alongside is my ten-year-old son, Danny."

"Where are they? What happened?"

"They're gone," Dan said, staring into the firelight. "Richmond, Virginia. That's where they went. She . . . she said that this was no place to raise a kid."

He poured another full glass of whiskey and John looked away as his brother continued. "She was right, you know. It's hell on women. But . . . but what else could I do but stay? I'm a Texas Ranger, man! I'm proud of that, and it *means* something."

"I know."

"Don't look so sad, Johnny. I'm doing what I was meant to do, and it's all I'm good at. I can plan campaigns and lead men into skirmishes and then bring 'em out alive."

"Sure you can," John said, trying to sound enthusiastic.

"Yeah. I've saved plenty of men. Just . . . well, I just wish I could have saved my marriage and grown old knowing my son. But—but I ain't good with women, John. And I couldn't quit the Texas Rangers. I'd have died inside." He looked up with bloodshot eyes. "Can you understand what I'm saying?"

John nodded heavily. "Maybe Linda will change her mind and return."

"Maybe," Dan conceded, without real hope. "But first, I have to make this country safe to raise a family. Then good folks might start coming in faster, to build schools and churches instead of gambling halls and saloons. It's a tough job. We need more good men. Men like you, John. Help us! Become a Texas Ranger and we'll ride together, side by side."

It was the hardest thing he'd ever done in his life, but John shook his head. "I wanted to join you before. I begged you. But now . . . now, I've learned the law and I mean to practice it without a gun."

"You won't join?" Dan was disbelieving.

"No."

The Ranger's mouth crimped. "Maybe that's best. You and me are all that's left and if we both get ambushed . . ."

John couldn't bear the thought. "Are you worried about the Cavendish gang?"

"Yeah." Dan swilled a mouthful of whiskey. Choked it down hard. "The bastards! They come out of nowhere. Strike. Then vanish. I don't even know where they hole up."

"The sheriff says they're the ones who hit the stage today."

"Bull!" Dan roared. "The Cavendish gang doesn't rob stages. They gobble up entire ranches. There's two hundred of them, not four. I tell you, he's got an army."

He took another long drink and shook his head in dejection. "What do I have? Ten men? Twenty? I don't know, because I can't keep them anymore, what with all the robbing, killing, and burning. We all know it's just a matter of time before we ride into a Cavendish trap."

John stood up and began to pace the floor. Fourteen years and nothing had changed. Nothing.

"Who is this Butch Cavendish, anyway?"

Dan snorted. "Butch Cavendish. Butch for butcher. He was a Major, *Union* Army. Fought at Missionary Ridge and Vicksburg. Dishonorably discharged. Ulysses Grant busted him for rape and murder. I hold Grant responsible for not hanging him on the spot. Hell, maybe it was all a Union plan anyway."

"What do you mean?"

"I mean Butch Cavendish is a goddamn Yankee officer leading an outlaw *army* in Texas!"

"You'll get him. The time will come when you'll get more help."

Dan swirled the amber fluid in his glass until it spilled on his clothes. "You gonna see him when he arrives?"

"Cavendish is coming *here?*"

"Hell, no! He knows I'd shoot him even if it took getting killed myself. I was talking about our great and bloody United States president, Grant. The bastard is coming here to make speeches and hunt buffalo. That's funny, ain't it?"

"What?"

"He says he wants to mend the nation. Put it together. And while he's doing it, he figures to slaughter Texas buffalo."

John turned away. He believed in the president. The country needed a strong leader now to reconstruct the south and put it back together again. But this sure wasn't the time or place to tell Dan his feelings.

"I'll leave the greetings to your citizens," John said quietly.

"Good. Happy you feel that way," Dan barked. "The whole town's gonna drive out and stand beside the railroad tracks. They're all packing food and little flags to wave. He's going to stop and eat something. Then make speeches about how he loves Texans."

Dan snickered. "I ain't going. If I did, I'd wave a Confederate flag and tell him what he can do with the Union."

"He *is* the President of the United States," John reminded.

"*Our* president is Jefferson Davis. Not Grant. Grant's a liar and a drunk. I say to hell with the president! And his cabinet, too. They don't give a damn for Texas and they ain't helping me. I've written letter after letter asking for more men and wages so I can stop Butch Cavendish from killing decent folks. Grant should have hung Cavendish! Then none of this would be happening."

"Dan, take it easy. You need some sleep. Get to bed."

"Sleep?" He smiled drunkenly. He closed his eyes and passed out cold.

It was almost daylight before John Reid could get to sleep, himself. He was consumed by the nightmare of what Butch Cavendish was doing—to Texas—to Captain Dan Reid.

He was killing them both.

Chapter 6

Sheriff Justin A. Wiatt had to face the townspeople of Del Rio and explain that the two outlaws, Stillwell and Gattlin, had escaped. A slip-up like this sure as the devil wasn't the kind of thing that would get him reelected next year; but then, he wasn't going to want the job if Butch Cavendish kept his promises.

Wiatt reined in his horse twenty miles north of Del Rio and slipped out of his saddle. He waited for almost an hour until he was sure no one was following him. He'd better hurry. Cavendish waited for no man.

The sun was almost straight up when Butch Cavendish stepped out into the compound with Sheriff Wiatt tagging along behind. Cavendish was a square-jawed man, wide and powerful in the shoulders and lean around the middle. At thirty-seven, everything about him suggested years of being in strict command of himself and others.

In contrast to his followers, he wore a suit and tie

and was immaculately groomed. Butch Cavendish knew he looked every inch a leader. He let everyone know that his orders were the law and failure to carry them out was punishable by death.

"Major Cavendish, sir," Wiatt called from behind, "don't you think this is going too far?"

Cavendish walked to the center of the compound. His pale gray eyes surveyed Stillwell and Gattlin. He noted the terror in their eyes as they sat tied in chairs with their mouths gagged. Cavendish turned away and nodded to one of his lieutenants. "You may begin."

"Detail, ten-shun!" The subordinate shouted the order, busting the stillness. The call echoed through the canyon. "Right face! March!"

An eight man detail moved like a well-oiled unit and Cavendish allowed himself a smile of approval. As a Union officer, he'd never commanded troops of this quality. But then he guessed money was a greater motivator than patriotism and ideals.

Cavendish waited until the detail was in position and at rest. He returned the lieutenant's salute and strode forward, hating the fact that the dust made a fine film on his polished boots.

"Dale Wesley Stillwell and Robert Edward Gattlin . . . it is the verdict of this military tribunal that you have each been found in violation of the Articles of War and the Soldier's Code of Conduct in that you failed in obedience to orders, and your undisciplined conduct resulted in the failure of a military objective. Therefore, it is the pronouncement of my tribunal that you be executed—by firing squad—forthwith." In a low voice, so no one else could hear, he whispered to the condemned men, "It will be quick. I *am* a merciful man and you must serve as an example to the others."

He did a perfect about-face.

"Mister Perlmutter."

"Sir!"

"Carry out the order of the tribunal."

"Yes, sir!"

Cavendish knew from experience that things would move quickly now. He made a mental note to reprimand whoever had gagged the pair. It had been done improperly.

"Atten-hut!"

The detail snapped erect. Eyes riveted to the front.

"Load and lock your weapons!"

Each man placed one bullet into the breech and snapped it shut in perfect unison.

"Major Cavendish, sir!"

His eyes did not move from the prisoners. "What is it, Sheriff?"

"Well . . . well, couldn't you just whip them or something, sir? I mean, they just did what ordinary men would have done."

Every eye in the compound rested on him, and Cavendish seemed to grow taller. His authority was being questioned; a perfect time to reinforce it in everyone's mind.

"Ordinary men?" he asked, rolling the words around his tongue and spitting them out. "I have no room for ordinary men, Mister Wiatt. None whatsoever!"

Now he was speaking to all of them, driving the fire of his zeal into their hearts. "Listen to me well. Each of you. We are embarked on a mission which will forever alter the course of American history. We are *not* ordinary men nor can there be any excuse for failure. Those who do not obey me and act, as these did, for their own personal gain, are a clear and present danger to each and every one of us—to our great destiny itself."

He scrutinized Sheriff Wiatt. "Do I make myself perfectly understood?"

"Yes, sir, Major Cavendish."

He turned toward the prisoners. Their eyes were dull and vacant.

"Proceed!"

"Yes, sir. Ready. . . . aim. . . . fire!"

The rifles exploded in unison, in a single cannon-like blast. Stillwell and Gattlin were lifted off the ground and hurled backward. They fell still, twisted in the Texas dirt.

The rifle fire echoed over and over against the walls of their canyon. Like applause, Cavendish thought.

John Reid stood beside Amy, Lucas and his brother, Dan, watching the fiesta. The plaza was filled with people celebrating All Saints Day with loud, happy music and dancing. Overhead, colorful lanterns swayed from the trees and Mexican children ran among the crowd or swung blindfolded at a candy-filled pinata. In the center of the plaza, a mariachi band was playing and the dancers swirled around them like brightly colored birds, graceful and proud.

Yes, this was a fiesta!

John smiled at Amy, "I want to compliment you on the story you wrote for your uncle's paper. I read it this morning."

She was pleased, appreciating his approval. "I'd like to be a newspaper editor some day. But there aren't many of them who are women."

"Well," John said, "then you can be one of the first, and a really good one, I'm thinking. But that article sure made me sound like a hero."

"You are."

He blushed and wanted to steer the subject away from himself. "Mister Striker, that was a very powerful editorial about the Cavendish gang."

"I liked it too," Dan interrupted sharply. "You've got courage, Lucas. If more folks spoke up, we could put an end to Butch Cavendish and his murdering army."

The editor nodded. "We *will* stop him, Captain. And, as for the editorial, well, it's the duty of an editor to expose that breed of man as far and wide as he can. I couldn't have remained silent. A good newspaper will not be intimidated."

He pulled his watch out of his vest pocket. "Which reminds me, Amy, I left our old Gutenberg in about twenty pieces at the office. Hidalgo is trying to put it all back together again. His family is here and I know he'd like to join them. I'd better go help. Be back soon."

John saw the worry in Amy's face. "You love him a great deal. Enough to worry."

She laughed nervously and smoothed her dress. "I didn't realize it showed so plainly. Yes, I do love my uncle and I'm concerned because he works too hard. Speaks out too openly."

"Maybe he has to."

"Probably. But, well, there's more. He's so committed to writing the truth—about anything—especially about how poor a job our sheriff is doing dealing with the Cavendish gang. It's almost become an obsession."

John understood perfectly. "My brother is the same way, Amy. This whole thing is tearing him apart."

In spite of the music and gaity around them, their admissions had dampened their spirits.

"Nice party," John offered.

"Yes. Do you dance?"

"Not very well, I'm afraid."

She was trying to snap them out of their mood. "Perhaps you need a lesson."

"Maybe I do," he answered, leading her out onto the dance floor. They stopped in one corner, out of the swirl of things. "Now what?"

"We dance," Amy said lightly.

He tried his best and she seemed to enjoy it. Even so, it was clear to John that Amy Striker was a *very* good dancer.

"How long have you been dancing?"

She looked up into his face. "Longer than you, but you're a fast learner. So am I, John. Ever since I was a little girl, I've been learning all the things a woman is supposed to know in order to be a perfect wife. Cooking, dancing, sewing. I can pass all the wifely tests with my eyes closed."

He detected a note of sarcasm. "But you don't care. Am I correct?"

"Yes," Amy smiled happily. "You're not only smart and brave, but also perceptive, John Reid. I'd better be careful around you. I'm just not interested in becoming someone's wife. Not yet, anyway."

"So what happens in the meantime?"

She snuggled in his arms. "I'm content being your dance partner."

The music ended and they left the floor. Amy gazed out at Del Rio and sighed, "It's easy to see why Uncle Lucas loves this town."

"A lot is happening out west, Amy. It's the birth of an era. There'll never again be such a growing, expanding time in our history."

"I know. Back east, big factories are producing machinery and equipment which will be brought out here and change all of this."

"True, but the west will be built by settlers, Amy. By their sweat and blood—not by machines. And people like your uncle and my brother will make it safe for everyone."

She looked at him with almost a quizzical expression. "You know, it's funny how you never speak of your own role, John. I have a feeling that you—more than anyone in Del Rio—are going to shape our destiny."

He laughed aloud and blushed with embarrassment.

"Go ahead and make fun. But I rarely miss when I have a strong feeling about a person."

He grew somber and uneasy. "Amy, I don't know why you're saying those things—especially right now. You see, when I returned, I thought I'd simply hang my shingle and practice law."

"And now?"

"I don't know," he admitted. "I believe in the law, what it stands for and how it brings out the decency in man and furthers his civilization."

"But sometimes it doesn't work very well," she said firmly. "Maybe because of crooked sheriffs and judges. Maybe because people like Butch Cavendish live by their own rules."

"Then we *make* it work better. We don't throw out what's good because of what's bad." He took a deep breath. "But what tears me apart is watching my brother try to work within the law and get no help."

"Things will change, John. And soon. You'll be a part of it, I'm certain."

"And so will you."

She shook her head, "I'm . . . I'm afraid not."

"What do you mean?" He felt an ominous warning.

"I'm here only for a while," she explained, avoiding his eyes. "I've accepted a reporter's job on the San Francisco *Chronicle*."

John felt as though the bottom of his dreams had fallen away. He tried to smile. "Congratulations, Amy."

Her eyes misted. "Oh, John. Hurry," she ordered, turning away quickly. "The music has started, and I feel like dancing with you."

He took her into his arms. Held her close. Not a man to give up on anything in life, he was wondering how he could change Amy's plans and make her stay. Del Rio, Texas needed her a whole lot more than San Francisco.

Lucas Striker bent over the heavy Gutenberg printing press and nodded with satisfaction. "Okay, Hidalgo," he said with a broad grin, "let's see if yesterday's front page comes out this time."

The Mexican nodded, pulled the heavy lever and the plate came down. A moment later, they were staring at the front-page headlines.

71

CAVENDISH!
OUTLAW GANG TRIES FOR STAGE.
ONE PASSENGER DEAD.
TWO OUTLAWS KILLED, TWO CAPTURED.
SHOTGUN GUARD CHARLES CASSIDY MURDERED!

Lucas looked to his assistant. "A headline like this has got to stir up some trouble. But we can't lose our courage, Hidalgo, we can't get scared into printing lies."

The front door swung open and six hooded men stood outside in frozen, deadly silence.

Hidalgo drew his hunting knife and stepped forward.

"No, Hidalgo, it's me they want. Not you." Lucas faced the line of hooded assailants. "Let this man go. I'm the editor and solely responsible for my paper's contents."

The two men in the center looked at each other for a moment. "All right," came the muffled answer. "But first, tell your Mexican to drop that pig-sticker and walk out slowly."

"No, señor," Hidalgo pleaded.

"Do it!" the editor insisted. "For God's sake, Hidalgo! Think of your wife. Of Donita."

"Si, Mister Striker." He dropped the knife and reluctantly moved forward. As he passed between them, two of the hooded figures lifted their pistols and hit him across the skull.

"Hey! You—"

Lucas jumped for them and the four outlaws were ready with their boots and fists.

John and Amy strolled hand in hand around the plaza. He stopped and took her into his arms. Before she knew what was happening, he was kissing her tenderly.

"You're not really going to San Francisco, are you?"

"I've got to. Oh, John, don't make this any harder for me than it is already."

"But why go? If you want to be a reporter, you can be one right here in Del Rio."

She pulled back, her eyes mirroring her uncertainty. "And if I did that, I'd *never* fulfill my dream of working on a big newspaper. Some day I will come back to Texas and start one of my own."

"Change your dream, Amy. Perhaps it wasn't meant to be. Maybe there's something better for you here."

"Like you?"

He nodded, realizing he was a fool to be talking this way. After all, he'd only just arrived in Del Rio. It would take time to get himself established; it would be a while before he could support a wife.

"Don't you see, John, I'd always wonder if I could have been a big city reporter. If I stay in Del Rio, I'll just be my uncle's helper. *He's* the editor and that's as it should be. I'd . . ." she searched for the words. "I'd just be an editorial assistant, a pleasant helpmate all my life."

John let her go. She meant every word she'd said and he understood her fear of losing her dream.

"How long would you have to work for the *Chronicle?*"

"Oh, I don't know. A year. Maybe two."

"That's not so bad. Probably take a man like myself at least that long to establish a practice."

He pulled a book out of his inside coat pocket. "I've got a little present for you."

Her eyes widened. "You . . . it's your copy of Miss Jackson's *Century of Dishonor!* Oh, John, I couldn't!"

"Sure you can, and you will. There are some passages that I've underlined. If you string them all together, they'll give you my reasons why you should hurry back to me and Texas." He tried to smile. "Will you write me from San Francisco?"

"Every day."

"And send me anything you've written? Stories. Articles. Book reviews."

She nodded and bit her lip.

"So," she said quietly, "let's enjoy the time we have left."

As their lips met, a scream filled the plaza and the music went dead.

"Hidalgo! In the name of God, Hidalgo!"

He staggered under the swaying lamps, clutching his stomach. He toppled face down on the dance floor and a Mexican woman smothered him with her tears.

Chapter 7

JOHN, Dan, and a half-dozen other Texas Rangers found the front door of the newspaper office open. The old printing press was overturned in the middle of scattered type and broken furniture. Papers were strewn everywhere. They all gaped in silence at the body of Lucas Striker hanging by a noose from the rafter.

"Uncle Lucas!" Amy screamed from outside.

"Don't let his niece in here!" Dan snapped. He quickly righted an overturned chair and hurriedly scrambled up to lower the body.

John rushed to shield the sight. She gasped, then buried her head on his shoulder. Her entire body was shaking uncontrollably, the sobs coming from deep inside. What kind of men could do this? Animals! Animals who needed to be stopped before they killed more decent people. The Cavendish Gang didn't rate the luxury of a trial. They deserved quick death. No more. No less.

Amy's wrenching sobs finally abated and she clung to him a long time before she could speak. The voice he heard was filled with bitterness. "John, I tried to warn him not to keep printing his editorials about Butch Cavendish and his gang. Over and over, I begged him to temper them—but he refused.

"John, I loved my uncle. He was good and brave. Where was your law when *he* needed it?"

"Captain Reid! We found six pairs of tracks out back."

"Mount up, rangers!"

John watched the Texas Rangers spring for their horses.

"All he ever lived for," Amy said brokenly, "was his newspaper. He believed in it so much. And he was a threat to Cavendish's brand of murder and intimidation. Is that what our so-called western justice is all about?"

"No." He gently pushed Amy away. "I'm taking your uncle's horse and riding with my brother."

He placed a finger over her lips. "Perhaps *I* was wrong, Amy. Some things just aren't the way they are described in books."

She nodded. Squeezed him tight, then let him go. Amy understood. "Please come back," she whispered.

Dan watched him mount the editor's horse. "Where do you think you're going?"

"With you."

"You sure?"

"I'm dead sure."

A flush of pride lit the ranger's tired face. "Damn, it's good to hear you say that!"

Dan sat erect in his saddle and spoke to his Texas Rangers. "This time, we're not quitting until we bring Cavendish and his killers to justice—the same brand of justice they gave Lucas Striker tonight. There'll be no quarter given or expected. Are my orders clear?"

They shouted their approval in a single, strong voice.

"Then let's go a-huntin', Texas Rangers!"

A dozen rangers fanned out across the prairie. Across the land lit by the moon, each man rode separate and deep within his own thoughts. This time there would be no compromise, no quitting the chase until the killers of Lucas Striker were eliminated and the grip of Butch Cavendish broken.

And John Reid was one of them. Riding stirrup-to-stirrup with the man he admired more than all others. Riding tall and proud. He would never hold Amy again until he could tell her that Del Rio and the Texas border was safe. And that, thanks to Texas Rangers, families could grow without fear—to build churches and schools and live their own hard-won dreams. Yes! And it would all be possible because of men who would fight for right—and the courtrooms be damned!

Several hours before daylight, they arrived at a stream, and Collins dismounted to check the tracks. Dan told him that Collins wasn't fast with a gun, but he was the best the company had when it came to reading tracks.

"They're still going north, Captain," Collins said. "One of their horses is limping on his right foreleg, but they're pushing hard."

"Deeper and deeper into Indian country."

"Yes, sir. And they ain't worrying about their back trail none. This is like tracking an elephant in snow."

"How far ahead?"

"An hour. Five minutes, more or less."

John could feel the soreness from a long night of riding, but he pushed the discomfort away and focused his attention on the first tinges of color on the horizon. The landscape grew brighter and brighter with every mile-eating stride. Suddenly the sun seemed to sprout from the earth and send brilliant gold and red streaks of color racing in their direction. It lifted off the horizon and glowed fiercely, lighting the buttes and hills in a spectacular golden brilliance. Magnificent!

At midmorning they halted. For hours they had silently followed the trail of the outlaws. They stopped where the tracks led straight into a tall, narrow-sided canyon.

"It's open at the other end," Dan said quietly. "I've been down through it before, and my stomach tightened like a Comanche drum. They call it Bryant's Gap. It's a natural ambush."

He fished a pair of binoculars from his saddlebags and searched the canyon. Dan took his time and nobody rushed him as the binoculars slid over every inch of the canyon wall.

"Nothing moves; there's not a sign of a living thing."

"Captain, sir."

"Speak up, Collins. Have I missed anything?"

"No, sir. It's just that, with your permission, I'd like to volunteer to ride in and check things out."

Dan scowled but there was pride in his voice. "It's beyond the call of duty, Collins. I can't let you do it alone."

"Beg your pardon, sir. But I'm the tracker here. If I see signs that they've abandoned the trail to hide, I'll come riding out fast."

There was a long pause. John could tell his brother didn't like it. He probably figured *he* should be the one to go in alone. But he realized that his men depended on his leadership.

"All right," Dan said, hesitantly. "Go ahead. But no heroics. Just watch yourself!"

Collins smiled bravely. "I always do, Captain."

They watched him ride in and John said, "He's a pretty brave man. Where'd you find him?"

"He found us. Just showed up about a month ago and said he wanted to be a Texas Ranger. He had a first-class outfit and I liked his appearance. You get so you can tell a man's worth by the looks of him and his belongings. Well," he grunted, "all my rangers got sand. Collins knows that. Reckon he's thinkin' he needs to prove himself in front of the others. It's a matter of personal pride."

"I hope," John said, "he gets the chance to live long enough to enjoy his new-found respect."

The minutes dragged on as they observed Collins' slow advance up the canyon. Dan took a bite of beef jerky and offered some to John. "I hate this waiting," he grumbled.

"Helps to talk about something else," John said, chewing mightily. "When was the last time you saw your boy, Danny?"

The captain's face softened. "Two years ago," he said easily. "I miss him, but we write often."

He turned in the saddle. "Listen, John, if anything should . . . well, you know, happen to me . . ."

"Dan, that's . . ."

"It's likely as not, brother. So let me finish. I want you to check on my son. Watch out for him and see that he turns out all right. A boy needs a father."

John remembered how much he needed his own father. "Yes, Dan, I'd watch out for your boy. That's a promise."

The brothers turned their attention once again to the canyon.

"There! I just saw Collins giving the signal that all is clear. He's coming back now."

John felt the relief run through all of them.

"Catch," Dan yelled.

John caught the silver badge that was a Texas Ranger Star.

"Pin it on, brother. I should have given it to you earlier. That badge gives you license to shoot outlaws. I don't have to tell you the tradition it carries. A lot of the best men in Texas have died defending its honor."

"Thank you," he whispered.

"You'll earn it," Dan vowed. "And you'll need this." From his saddlebags he produced a gun.

"I guess I might be a bit rusty," John said, hefting its weight and appreciating its balance.

"Maybe. But you were damn good with a rifle. It'll come back fast."

John pinned the star on his chest and looked up into his brother's eyes.

"You'll do, John Reid. You'll do mighty fine!"

They passed into Bryant's Gap in complete silence. The air was hot and still and John felt the sweat erupt from his body as he studied the overhanging cliffs.

The canyon suddenly widened and each of the twelve Texans scanned the towering cliffs with a penetrating intensity. Nothing.

Halfway in, the brothers checked their horses and suddenly John's heart began pounding wildly. In that one, chilling moment, he just *felt* something was wrong.

"Dan," he whispered urgently.

His brother jerked around in the saddle. Dan's eyes were wild. "Collins!" he shouted. "Where is Collins!"

Each ranger looked to the man behind and, when their heads swung back to their leader, they all felt the wind of death blow against their cheeks.

"We were led into a trap!" Dan yelled. "Let's get the hell out of here!"

Eleven men wheeled their horses and sank spurs. From high above on both sides of the canyon's rim, a hundred and more rifles began exploding down into the canyon.

Then came the boulders. Huge, lumbering boulders hurtling down the cliff, at the gap's opening! Dear God, he prayed, they are sealing our coffin!

Chapter 8

JOHN could hear his brother shouting, but he could not distinguish the words through the deafening thunder of the tumbling rocks. He knew they were being slaughtered, crushed by the giant boulders that sent a great cloud of dust into Bryant's Gap. The men and horses were a swirling mass of death and confusion.

John tried to find a target, but it was hopeless. Their ambushers were on the canyon's rim and the ranger's pistols were no match against the deadly Cavendish rifles.

Dan's voice broke through the confusion. "This way, John! Follow me, rangers!"

There were few alive to hear the desperate command. John tried and, for a moment, as his mount lunged forward, it seemed that the gap appeared just ahead. Then his mount froze in mid-stride and collapsed.

Instinct saved him from going down under the dying animal. He jerked his feet out of the stirrups and threw his body out of the saddle. John struck his shoulder

85

and rolled over and over. But he came up with his revolver blazing.

A ranger fell as lead drove through his upper leg. John grabbed him and they scrambled for cover.

"Hi, kid," the wounded ranger shouted over the volleying gunfire. "How do you like being one of Texas' finest?"

John lifted his head. "Right now, words seem inadequate to express my feelings," he deadpanned.

The ranger, whose name was Stephenson, grinned, lifted the rifle he'd managed to hang onto, and edged it around the boulder. He fired and, instantly, a dozen pieces of lead exploded off their covering rock.

"Yeah," he grunted, squeezing the bullet wound in his leg, "it's a great life, all right. Hell, stick around for when things really get exciting!"

"I'll try," John gritted, firing without hope.

"I been around a long time, kid," Stephenson choked. "Defended San Antone with Big Sam Houston. Fought alongside McCulloch in the war with Mexico . . . rode with Kit Carson and John Coffee Hays. And this is the most excitin' of all."

He fired again. Twice, and fast. When he ducked back, there was a bitter grin on his lips. "I got one of the bastards! Knocked him plumb off the rim."

Stephenson ducked back out to fire. "There's one right—ahhh!"

The bullet kicked him around in a circle and John leapt to pull him back. In the next instant, he felt as though a cattle's branding iron was searing his flesh.

"Stephenson!" he choked, dragging the man and himself to cover as a hail of lead bit the earth all around. "Stephenson!"

But the old Texas Ranger couldn't answer. He'd finally gotten a gut's worth of excitement.

Dan Reid and Ranger Charles Palmer were the only two horsemen who escaped through the gap alive.

"Goddamn, we made it Captain. We *made* it!"

Dan knew he'd been hit twice, but neither wound was fatal. Dan's eyes combed the dusty gap. Each second felt like an hour. He prayed for others to come through—for his brother John to be spared.

"Where are they?"

Palmer swallowed. "I saw Lopez go down under a boulder. Flattened him and his horse. Alcott died with a bullet in the back, Rankin took one in the stomach, and Little, Stacy, and Karner died in that first volley. Sir," Palmer whispered, "there ain't no one else coming out."

"No!" Dan cried. "It can't be true!"

"Captain . . ."

They both heard a fresh round of gunfire.

"See! I told you. If there's only one left, it's *got* to be my brother. John is alive!"

"Sir . . ."

Dan's eyes sparked with hope and intensity as he reloaded his gun. "You can stay here, ranger. Stay and find Collins. That bastard was Cavendish's man all the time. He led us into a death trap! Find him and kill him, Palmer!"

"Yes, sir. But Captain, it ain't in me to let you ride back through that gap alone."

Dan looked up. He seemed to realize for the first time that he was not alone. "Do you realize what you're saying, Charley?"

Charles Palmer straightened and reloaded his own weapon. "I know. I'm going with you. It could have been me inside there."

"Then let's ride for the glory of Texas—for her Rangers!"

And they charged into the canyon of death with frozen grins on their rugged faces and hot-barreled six-guns in their fists.

They exploded through the mouth of the gap and

scattered in every direction. Charles Palmer died instantly as a rifle slug threw him out of his saddle. His boot clung to one stirrup, and his lifeless body bounced across the canyon floor.

From deep in the canyon, John saw his brother coming. He tried to give him covering fire. With a gun in each hand, he leaped out from behind the boulder and shot at the canyon rims as fast as he could pull the trigger. It was hopeless. Dan's mount squealed and went down hard, flinging its rider to the ground.

John's guns were empty and he started to run towards his brother.

"No!" the captain yelled. "John, go back!"

A slug ate into John's thigh and he felt his legs go out from under him. He could hear the bullets striking the rock floor. Somehow, he managed to retain consciousness. He could see his brother crawling closer, struggling to save him.

"John!" the captain gasped, as the last piece of lead burned through his stomach. With the last of his strength, Dan smiled, a crooked and sad smile. "At least . . . at least, we did it together this time, little . . . brother, and you're gonna tell my son . . ."

Butch Cavendish lowered his special, high-powered hunting rifle and nodded with critical approval. "There isn't a finer weapon in the world. Paid two thousand dollars and had it custom made."

He gestured down at the slaughter. "Those last two shots into Captain Reid were perfect." His eyes finished their inspection. "Collins!"

"Yes, sir."

"Go down and check the bodies. I don't want a single one left breathing."

The betrayer paled. "Couldn't someone else, Major? I mean . . . I got to know them, sir, and . . ."

"Precisely," Cavendish spat. "You rode with the last of the Texas Rangers. Now go down and thank your luck not to be one of them!"

Collins nodded jerkily. "Yes, sir!" He wheeled his horse and hurried away. He reached the canyon's floor and moved slowly among the bodies. But he didn't touch them or look into their eyes.

Butch Cavendish watched the ex–Texas Ranger move squeamishly among the fallen.

"You know, Mister Perlmutter," he drawled, "it would seem too coincidental if the only surviving Ranger wasn't at least wounded."

His aide nodded. Understood perfectly. "Enough just to get back to town?"

"Yes. I think that would be fine, Perlmutter. Would you like to try my weapon?"

"Oh yes, sir!"

Cavendish handed over the rifle. It was long and sculptured; its polished walnut stock glistened in the sunlight. His eyes watched with professional detachment and approval as Perlmutter handled the weapon expertly and wasted no time in firing. It was all quite competently executed, he thought, as the rifle boomed.

"Did you hit your target?" he asked, feigning total indifference.

"Yes, sir."

"Very good, Perlmutter."

When they reached the canyon floor, Collins was in shock, with blood seeping from the wound. Cavendish rode over to the traitor.

"You had better start for town, Collins, or you'll bleed to death."

"Yes, Major!"

"If you make it back, present the right story. Otherwise, you will not live to enjoy the medal and speeches they'll most likely give you as the only survivor. Do you understand?"

"Yes, sir, Major Cavendish," he whispered.

"Good work, Collins." He dismissed the man with a

contemptuous smirk and waved to the army he commanded.

"Let's ride, my compatriots! Tonight, I will see that you have all the women and whiskey you want!"

Everyone was gone and the canyon was still—completely still except for the feeble, struggling beat of one man's heart.

Chapter 9

IT was very hot, as it had been the day before and the days before that. A solitary Indian watched a hawk float above the canyon, then dive with talons extended toward its prey. A hundred feet from the ground, the bird screeched and beat its great wings at the still, hot air then rose and flew away.

Tonto's eyes searched for the cause of the hawk's alarm. His face tightened and he rose from a crouch and moved swiftly to his brown and white pinto horse. There was a string of dead rabbits draped across Scout's withers, and he left them hanging as he mounted and rode toward the floor of the canyon.

He saw the tracks of many shod horses and knew at once that there had been trouble in the canyon. As he approached the bodies, he wondered how the famous Captain Dan Reid had allowed himself to be drawn into such a death trap. The Texas Rangers had been honorable and brave men who treated the People with respect and fairness.

Good white men deserved to be buried rather than have scavengers strip their bones. Tonto guided Scout among them, studying their death poses, noting the huge boulders and trying to recreate the violent struggle that must have taken place in a few short minutes. Tonto halted before the body of Captain Reid. As his

93

eyes looked toward the others, he heard a faint, muffled sound. It was a scraping sound almost like brush
across rock. Tonto found the noise and dismounted
quickly. He knelt beside the figure holding Dan Reid's
body and rolled him over. He stared at the pain-
wracked, dirt-streaked face and knew that the man was
still alive. It seemed impossible, yet as he pressed his
ear to the stranger's bloody shirt, Tonto detected a
heartbeat. He noticed something else, a piece of silver
jewelry under the shirtfront. Again, he studied the face
and his hand began to tremble. He ripped open the
shirt and rocked back on his heels.

The silver and turquoise amulet! "Trusted friend!"
he whispered fervently. "Kemo Sabe!"

Tonto waved his hunting knife over the flames until
its tip glowed. His dark, serious face glistened with
sweat as he turned to his unconscious friend and examined the wounded shoulder. He threw his head back
and called to the sky, asking the Great Spirit to guide
his knife well, that he might save his brother's life.
After several minutes, Tonto's expression became relaxed and his hand moved swifly and with rock-hard
steadiness.

The knife's blade sliced deep and then twisted and
probed until Tonto felt the blade touch the bullet.
John groaned deliriously, his body spasmed with agony
as Tonto held him still. Then, with a surgeon's touch,
he flicked the blade in a precise circular motion and the
lead slug popped free.

The bleeding was heavy now and the Indian moved
quickly. Ignoring his own pain, Tonto reached into a
boiling pot and grabbed a scalding handful of herbs.
When he rubbed them into his friend's shoulder, John
thrashed like a wild man. But, once more, Tonto held
him steady until the mass of sodden herbs stopped the
flow of blood. As the medicine cooled, John Reid
lapsed into a heavy sleep. Tonto watched his boyhood
friend, as his labored breathing gradually grew easier

and as his pulse began to strengthen. He stood and began the Dance of Healing. Tonto begged for forgiveness from the Great Spirit Healer because he was not a medicine man and had taken powers that were not his own.

As he danced and chanted, Tonto pledged his honor to the People and vowed that he would remain strong that he might give them more to eat. The last years had been very bad. And, as he carried on the ancient ceremony, Tonto asked the Spirit Healer to bring his trusted friend back to life that he might also help the People. As the hours passed, the Indian started to believe in his heart that John Reid's life had been returned by the Spirit Healer, he brushed his hand across his friend's brow and drove away all the evil fever.

"Dan," the half-delirious man called. "Dan!"

Tonto leaned forward. He wiped the perspiration from his friend's brow.

"Dan! Don't ride back. Dan, no!"

The eyes blinked open. They were desperate and pleading.

"Kemo Sabe. It is over. You must rest now."

John's vision focused. His body relaxed. "Tonto? Tonto, is that you?"

"It *is* Tonto."

John reached up. He tried to grip the Indian's hand but he was too weak. He closed his eyes and drifted into a peaceful sleep, while Tonto remained at his side in silent vigil and thanked the Spirit Healer for this gift of life.

He awoke at night to see Tonto squatting beside the fire, cutting meat. John stared at his Indian friend, remembering their parting fourteen years earlier. How tall and strong Tonto was now! His black hair hung shoulder-length with a feather on the right side. Gone was the small bow and arrow with which he'd become so expert as a child and, in its place, Tonto wore a holstered gun held by a bright red sash wrapped about his waist. The Indian was long-limbed and graceful, and his strong jawline and penetrating eyes made him a strikingly handsome warrior.

"You have changed," John said.

"So have you, Kemo Sabe. Much else has changed with the seasons, but it is not all good." Tonto poked at the fire. "I am sorry about your brother."

John nodded. He couldn't find his voice as he remembered vividly those last few seconds when he'd held the dying ranger.

"I buried him," Tonto said.

He opened a small bundle of belongings and John reached for them. His throat tightened until he could not swallow—could scarcely breathe. He held Dan's ranger star and the blood-stained neckerchief he'd used so desperately. There was one last memento. "His vest, Kemo Sabe."

John studied the pair of blood-crusted bullet holes that were only three or four inches apart. When he spoke, his voice was bitter and rich with the thirst for vengeance. "I saw the man who put these holes into Dan's chest."

"Butch Cavendish?"

"Yes. I've never seen him before, though I've heard descriptions. It *was* Cavendish and I swear he'll pay!"

"Cavendish is an evil man. He kills many," Tonto said.

John tried to sit up, but pain and Tonto's arresting hand forced him back.

"I'll find him, my friend."

Tonto nodded gravely. "I will help."

"No," John replied. "It's too dangerous."

He took John's hand. "We will help each other, Kemo Sabe."

"Yes!" John whispered. "We will ride together." Then his eyes closed and he fell into a deep and troubled sleep.

John Reid was shocked as they entered Tonto's

village. Fourteen years earlier, when he'd lived among them, the People had flourished and were both proud and happy. But now! Now, there were only a handful of teepees where once there had been more than a hundred. And the villagers who remained seemed broken and passive. He could feel the despair that hung like poisonous smoke over the village. The People were dying.

"Tonto, what happened?"

"Soldiers!" Tonto spat the word like an oath. "Soldiers who guard us that we might slowly die of hunger."

An old woman bustled defiantly toward the travois and stared at John with hate-filled eyes. Tonto barked sharply and the squaw left him alone.

Tonto dismounted and strode to his friend. "Kemo Sabe. A council is being held in this teepee. I go inside to speak for you. This is necessary."

John understood. "Tell them my heart is wounded by what I see. Remind them that I was once one of their children and have never forgotten their kindness. And do not let it go unsaid that I am proud to be your blood brother."

Tonto clasped his outstretched hand. "I will tell them these things," he promised.

Outside, John heard the conversation that took place between Tonto and a new chief.

"The white man gives us many promises, but keeps only one. They swore to take our land, and they took it. And its price? Look into the thin faces of our people, Tonto. You see only suffering and misery. Why then do you bring us one of the whites to make strong even as the People weaken?"

"Chief, no warrior has more reason to hate the whites than Tonto." There was a long pause. "For it was the whites that robbed me of happiness by taking my wife and child. But this man I bring is Kemo Sabe, my trusted friend. It is he who entered our camp fourteen winters ago and learned to respect our ways."

"It is he? Your blood brother?"

"Yes," Tonto said flatly. "And I will protect his life with my own. But if he betrays our People, then I, Tonto, will decorate my banner with his hair."

John heard the murmur of Indian voices, then Tonto's final words to the council. "But this man will never betray us. He is a friend and, together, we will ride to protect the rights of all people. Judge him not by his color, but by his heart. For he is Tonto's blood brother. Always!"

John Reid stood fifty feet from the target. It was a small piece of hide tacked on a tree, and he doubted he could even come close to hitting it left handed. Yet, he knew he must learn because the wound in his right shoulder might never heal completely. Before long, he'd rid himself of the sling. Perhaps, by then, he would be able to fire accurately with either hand.

The chief, seeing his concern and hesitancy, spoke. "You must recognize the Spirit that works within you."

He fired. Missed badly.

"For the Spirit will guide you in the ways of truth and will protect you even as you protect those in need. Listen to the Spirit—hear it whispering on the wind!"

This time, he raised the pistol and squeezed the trigger very slowly. Another miss. Yet, he knew it was closer.

"Each man chooses the place he will take in this world and the Spirit will guide him to this true destiny. For you, my adopted son, and for Tonto, your trusted friend, I will ask the Spirit to come and dwell in your hearts forever. He will guide you always and you will be strong for all peoples."

He fired, missed the target, but his slug ate some tree bark.

Tonto approached. "Kemo Sabe. Maybe you need a bigger target—like a sleeping buffalo."

John laughed, but it was a rusty sound without real humor. The memory of Bryant's Gap burned deep within his soul. He knew with certainty that he could never rest until Butch Cavendish and his gang were brought to justice.

John fired again but only nicked the target. In anger and frustration, he emptied the last two bullets, missing each time.

"Tonto, I once swore I'd never kill men with guns and now, I'm practicing with both hands and revenge in my heart."

He began to reload, but Tonto stepped closer and held out his palm. "Try these."

John stared at the silver bullets, then glanced up questioningly.

"They are more accurate, Kemo Sabe."

He reloaded. Took a deep breath and fired. The hide target jumped and there was no doubt he'd scored, as the Chief and a group of Indian children smiled with approval.

"I told you they'd make a difference," Tonto said, matter-of-factly. "Our tribal chiefs first used silver arrowheads; they flew straighter and longer and hunted as if they had eyes. Silver is pure. It has been a symbol of justice since the year of the sun.

"One day, Kemo Sabe, your bullet will pierce the heart of Butch Cavendish—and I will be with you to see your revenge."

John fired once more and his confidence grew. "Now that I can hit what I aim for, I must work on speed. First with the left, then my right hand. I *will* become a marksman with both and faster than any man I shall ever chance to face."

"It will come. But first, you must gain strength. To do this, we must walk."

John nodded and, together, they began another painful hike. Each day, they went a little farther. John traveled slowly and his limp was pronounced. Yet, he never complained, and Tonto was careful not to push him too long or hard.

It was mid-afternoon and the trail was steep. John's

teeth were gritted against the throbbing from his wounded thigh. "Is this one of your Indian tortures?"

"Walking is good for you, Kemo Sabe."

"Maybe. But you'll never get your tribe's vote as medicine man."

"You grow stronger."

"How strong do I have to be?" John gasped, nearly falling on the rough, wooded slope.

"Strong enough for Cavendish."

He took a deep breath. Tonto was right. "Keep walking," he said.

They were almost at the top when they heard a terrible piercing squeal.

"A horse!"

"No," Tonto said. "Buffalo!"

"Horse."

"Buffalo!"

Again the scream of rage and pain.

"This is no time to argue," Tonto said. "We shall see."

They came rushing out of the trees to a place where an underground spring fed the water-starved land.

"Look," Tonto breathed. "We were both right!"

"I don't believe my eyes!" John whispered. "A buffalo and a white stallion fighting to the death!"

Tonto nodded. "They fight for the water each must drink. Neither will give ground. Only one will survive."

Of course, John thought, in this country, water *was* life. He leaned forward intent on the battle being waged. The stallion, it seemed, could not win—not against the massive bull with its superior weight and sharp horns. Again and again, the bull charged, hooking viciously, trying to gore the stallion's soft underbelly, leaving bloody slashes along the silvery flanks.

The earth seemed to tremble under their stomping feet and both men admired the courage of these two magnificent animals. The stallion appeared to wait for the bull's charges, then it would whirl and lash out swiftly with all its might.

The white stallion was successfully countering the charges of its stronger opponent. John felt his pulse quicken as he gazed at the animal's long white mane and tail that flowed like a silver banner. But then, just as it seemed the buffalo was tiring, it hooked unexpectedly and the stallion went down thrashing.

John started to run, but Tonto gripped his arm. "No, Kemo Sabe! This battle must be finished!"

He hesitated, torn between his concern for so beautiful and courageous a horse and the realization that Tonto was right.

The stallion fought to regain its footing, as the bull whipped about and charged, intent on finishing the kill. At the very last moment, the horse scrambled erect and reared, snapping at the bull's neck with its teeth and clamping down like an empty bear trap.

"The fight is not over, Kemo Sabe. The stallion grows strong as the buffalo tires."

"Yes! But how can a horse possibly kill a bull that size?"

"I do not know."

Head down, the buffalo charged again. And, once more, the stallion barely avoided those deadly horns as it lashed out with its teeth and forelegs. The animals faced one another in the swirling dust.

The buffalo charged, only this time it seemed to realize it must bury its horns quickly. With instinctive cleverness, it hooked, then threw its tremendous bulk against the stallion, knocking it to the earth. The horse was halfway up as the bull wheeled and struck again. John winced when he heard the great white stallion's shriek of pain as it fell once more.

It would have died right then if its thrashing legs hadn't tripped the buffalo and sent it crashing to the ground, burying its killing horns in the sod. The buffalo rose slowly. The stallion reared and drove its sharp forefeet once again into his opponent. Twice, the gigantic bull tried to rise, but each time it was beaten to the dirt. Finally, it lay still.

With the last of its strength, the magnificent victor came down once more.

"Never," Tonto whispered, "in all the legends of the People, have I heard of such a battle. If I had not witnessed this with my own eyes, I would not have believed a horse could kill a buffalo."

"That's no ordinary horse," John whispered reverently as he moved forward.

"Don't get too close, Kemo Sabe. That's a demon."

But John wasn't listening as he slowly approached the stallion who watched him with defiant eyes.

"Easy, boy. I'm not going to hurt you. Easy, big horse," he said softly, then reached down tentatively and stroked the thick, muscled neck. He studied the wounds and saw that only a few were deep and all would heal.

"His legs are not broken," Tonto observed. "He will survive to fight again."

"Yes. But next time I hope he chooses something his own size. Look at him, Tonto! Isn't he magnificent!"

A shadow passed across the Indian's face. "Yes, but he is a killer horse."

As if he heard and understood, the white stallion suddenly lurched forward, knocking John to the ground. The horse rose on its hind legs and pawed the air above John. Tonto reached for his gun and cocked it to fire.

"No, Tonto!"

The stallion's hooves struck the earth beside John's face. For an instant, the animal's wild eyes penetrated his own. Once again, it reared and clawed at the air, its sleek coat shining like silver in the sun. But, instead of planting those deadly hooves into John's body, the stallion whinnied, turned, and galloped away. Its mane and tail streamed majestically behind it.

John rose shakily and watched the white horse disappear.

"I'm going to ride him!" he whispered fervently.

Chapter 10

It was a quiet afternoon, and John swam in the mountain river feeling refreshed and optimistic about his recovery. Each morning he spent hour after hour of hard, concentrated work practicing the draw and fire with his two guns. Each afternoon, sore and reeking of gunpowder, he would go for a swim.

As his fingers touched the bank, John noticed the huge shadow on the surface of the river. He looked up and saw the great white stallion prancing and shaking its head in play.

"Well, good morning!"

The stallion whinnied, pawed the air, and galloped away into the forest.

"You'll be back!" John yelled as he left the water and headed for his belongings. He glanced where the stallion had gone and felt a surge of excitement. There seemed to be an understanding between them that transcended mere curiosity.

John remembered the chief's prophesy about the

Spirit and couldn't help but think that he and the horse were part of something beyond his immediate understanding.

Later that evening, John sat beside the campfire and studied the blood-stained vest of his brother. With his mind filled with memories of Dan, his fingers poked through the closely spaced bullet holes.

For a moment, he stared at them, then glanced over at Tonto who was braiding a new lariat. "My friend, I've just realized that I can't appear as John Reid anymore. If I'm to get Cavendish, he and his followers must believe they've killed *all* of the Rangers."

He thought of Amy Striker and realized the implication of his next words—how heavily he must pay for them. "Tonto, since I'm going to devote my life to bringing murderers like Butch Cavendish to justice, I can't let it be known that I'm John Reid. To the world, he died with the other Texas Rangers."

Tonto nodded in understanding. "We must return to Bryant's Gap and dig your grave, Kemo Sabe."

That last morning before riding out of Tonto's village, the Indian tied a hide target to a tree.

"Kemo Sabe, the time has come for you to know your own skill. I have placed six arrows through the target. You have twelve silver bullets in your guns. For each bullet, there is an arrowhead or the bright shaft-feathers. Show me and the People what you have learned."

John stepped away from his friend. His fingers shadowed the handles of the pistols. He drew in one smooth, fast motion. His hands were a blur as he whipped the twin Colt .45's up, roaring lead and smoke. The arrows shattered at each end and, when the air cleared and the thunder of gunfire died, not a single feather or arrowhead remained intact.

"Now you are ready, Kemo Sabe."

John reloaded his guns with silver bullets, knowing

that the next time he fired, it would be at Butch Cavendish. "Thanks. I couldn't have made it alone."

The Indian watched him closely. "I know what burns in your heart, my friend. But I, too, have a need for vengeance."

"Tell me," he said.

Tonto's face was rigid with bitterness. "I remember the People starving in winter. And how the soldiers came and killed my wife and son. I . . . have a sickness inside like you, remembering how the soldiers' bullets cut down my people."

John's hand came to rest on his blood brother's wide shoulder. "You and I, we cannot bring those we loved back to life. All we can do is to prevent others from feeling our pain. You have pledged to help me, and I give you my pledge that I will fight to save the People."

"To the death?"

John nodded.

Tonto smiled knowingly. "Two dreams become one. Our trails will never cross but always run side by side."

As they had done years ago, the two men clasped hands. They were blood brothers and that would *never* change as long as they lived.

"Look at him!" John exclaimed, as the great white stallion entered the clearing.

"He shines like the moon."

"Like silver," John whispered, moving toward the horse. *Never* had he seen anything to match this animal's beauty and power. The stallion moved so gracefully, the muscles rippling under its shiny white coat.

"Easy, boy," John called, his voice low and soothing. "Easy. That's it, nobody wants to hurt you, big fella."

The stallion reared, but its ears were forward rather than back, and John knew he was being tested by the great horse.

"Just you and me," he murmured. "No one else."

The stallion lolled its head, nickered softly as John's

fingers touched its powerful neck. Then, when he moved closer, the animal bolted and ran.

"Silver!"

The majestic stallion plowed the earth with its hooves as it came to a halt.

"Don't run, Silver!"

The horse edged forward, magnetized by the human walking in its direction. Tonto followed behind John, carrying blankets, hackamore, and saddle.

"Easy, horse. Listen to the Spirits. They bring us together," John whispered, as the two met once again in the clearing. And, this time, when the tall, broad-shouldered man reached out, the stallion did not run. Instead, it stood quivering with excitement as though it had been sired for this moment in time.

John reached behind without looking and took the blanket from Tonto while he stroked the stallion's neck. "This isn't going to hurt you, big fella—but it might kill me."

He gently slipped one of the blankets over the stallion's trembling head, his voice never losing its soothing quality. With great care, Tonto saddled the animal, while John placed the hackamore over the muzzle and ears.

John could feel the excitement building inside both of them as he prepared to mount. With the reins laced through his fingers, he gripped the saddlehorn, took a deep breath, and nodded to his waiting friend.

"Let him go!"

Tonto yanked the blanket off the white head as John mounted. For one moment, Silver stood rigid and unmoving. Then, without warning, the majestic animal reared, its hooves beating at the sun, a shrieking cry in its mighty throat.

John was certain the stallion was going to fall over backward—so certain that he almost kicked free of the stirrups and jumped away. But Silver did not go over, as he walked on his back legs and fought the weight that clung to his back. His hooves stomped the ground and he bucked, throwing John forward and across the powerful neck. Then the stallion wheeled in two complete circles. John clung desperately to his flowing mane. *Never* had he been jolted and wrenched so violently!

Silver lurched forward, snapping his rider's spine like a whip. John hung on with all his strength as the animal began to race across the landscape. Their speed was awesome, and the horse blistered the land, leaping gulleys and brush, swerving at the last instant around trees, charging headlong up steep trails that seemed impossible to climb. The wind stung John's eyes, and his hat blew away in those first tremendous strides. But he hung on, feeling the blood pound in his ears and knowing if the mighty horse lost its footing, they would never rise again.

Finally, John detected a gradual slackening of the pace, and he began to assume control by tightening his hold on the reins—not hard or viciously—just enough to let the stallion know he wanted to be its friend rather than master.

Suddenly, there was a cliff looming just ahead! "Whoa, Silver!" he yelled.

It was too late. John felt the animal gather itself and the next instant they were airborne, hurtling into empty space. They were plunging toward the watery gorge. John saw the river blasting up to meet them, then felt a tremendous jolt as they were covered by a shower of water. He was thrown sideways and scraped over submerged boulders by underwater currents. A red haze filled his brain and his lungs cried out for air as he clawed desperately toward the surface. Just as he began to inhale water, his face burst up to the sky, and it was as though he'd been reborn. He paddled feebly to shore and lay in the shallow water, gasping for a long, long time. When his vision cleared, he realized he was laying beside the forelegs of the white stallion.

John pushed himself to his feet. He stood, weak and

battered. "You're gonna have to do better than that," he whispered shakily.

The white stallion nuzzled him roughly, and John grabbed the saddle to keep from falling over. He gathered up the reins and placed his hand on the saddlehorn.

"Are we going to do it all over again, big Silver? Any more surprises?"

As if understanding the man's words, the animal shook its head playfully as John hauled into the saddle. He didn't know what to expect this time, but realized he couldn't withstand another round of punishment like the one he'd just undergone.

Maybe Silver realized it, too, for he patiently waited until John was seated, then let himself be guided by the reins.

"Thanks," John whispered, leaning forward to pat the muscular neck. "You won't regret this, Silver. The Spirit has brought us together, and together we will ride the justice trail."

He towered beside the line of graves while Tonto held Silver and Scout. Now there was one more grave —his own.

John took a deep breath and stared at it. "Let Cavendish and all men think that I died here with the Rangers. With my brother."

"Dan," he said, kneeling beside his brother's grave. "I'll see that your boy is well taken care of as long as I am alive. And I swear to you, wherever your murderers are, however long it takes, I *will* find them. What Cavendish and men like him owe you, they will pay in full. *To this I pledge my life!*"

He stood, placed his hat back on, and slowly turned to face his Indian friend. He wore a black leather mask —soaked wet with his own tears and Captain Dan Reid's blood.

Tonto shivered and stared in awe at the Lone Ranger.

Tonto's chin lifted with pride. "The mask is good, Kemo Sabe. It will protect you from enemies until the day we strike at Cavendish. But what then? After he has paid for your brother's life with his own?"

"I will wear it always," the masked man said quietly, sadly remembering his dreams. It seemed like a long time ago that he'd thought of being a frontier lawyer and a husband to Amy Striker.

He studied the graves a final time, and his eyes came to rest on his own marked cross. "I am the last of them all, Tonto. I *am* the Lone Ranger!"

Tonto stretched out his hand to this man who had suffered as deeply as himself. His voice was thick with emotion. "Kemo Sabe."

"Trusted friend," the Lone Ranger whispered, "let's ride!"

They swung into the saddle and raced out of the death-trap canyon. The masked rider, the hope of the frontier, was born at Bryant's Gap.

Chapter 11

THE Lone Ranger and Tonto tied their horses at the hitching post in front of Sheriff Justin A. Wiatt's office. The hour was late and few people were about.

"Cover me, Tonto," he said, striding to the door and pushing it open. Wiatt and his deputy glanced up from their newspaper.

"Who the hell are you!" Wiatt snarled.

The deputy eased his fingers closer to his holstered gunbutt. "Anyone who walks into a sheriff's office wearing a mask better have a damned good reason!"

"I do." His eyes fell on the headline they'd been studying so intently. As he read it his heart expanded with pride for Amy.

CAVENDISH STILL AT LARGE
WHEN WILL THIS KILLER BE CAUGHT?

He motioned toward the paper. "Where is he?"

"Who?" the Sheriff asked.

"Don't play games with me. I want Cavendish."

Wiatt bristled. "Mister, if you're a bounty hunter, I handle that line of work in Del Rio, so ride out while you still can."

"Maybe he's looking to join up with Cavendish," the deputy snarled, easing to one side and bracing his feet apart. "Take your mask off—now!"

Tonto slipped into the doorway. He cocked his gun and aimed it at the deputy's badge.

"It won't be necessary for me to take off my mask," the Lone Ranger said quietly, as the deputy threw his hands aloft.

"I want to know where Cavendish was last seen and if he's been raiding lately."

Wiatt looked worried, but he was the law and that reinforced him enough to snap, "You ask a lotta questions for a masked man. But since that injun has the drop on us, I'll answer. We don't know where Cavendish is or I'd be after him right now with a deputized posse."

"You'd do nothing," came the contemptuous reply. "Now just a damned . . ."

The masked man took a step forward, and Wiatt swallowed whatever it was he almost damned.

"Where's the only man who survived the Bryant's Gap massacre? His name is Collins."

"What do you want to know about him for?"

"He's an old friend. We rode together once."

"Probably find him in the cantina," the deputy said nervously, ignoring the cold look from his boss.

The Lone Ranger glanced at Tonto. This interview was over—for now. But he suspected Wiatt was going to have to do a lot of explaining.

"Say!" Wiatt called, as the Lone Ranger walked out the door. "Whoever you are, masked man, I want to know just exactly what you want with Butch Cavendish!"

The Lone Ranger's eyes burned through the bullet

holes. Then, without a word of explanation, he motioned to Tonto and they departed, leaving the pair of
lawmen staring at the door.

On the way to the cantina, they passed the *Del Rio
Register & Dispatch* office on the opposite side of the
street. A lamp flickered in the window, and the Lone
Ranger halted in midstride in front of the freshly
painted sign—AMY STRIKER, EDITOR. Then the lamp
was extinguished, and he watched her leave the building, lock the newspaper office, and turn to walk down
the shadowy street.

"I knew you'd stay, Amy," he said sadly, feeling the
loss deep inside his chest. Had things worked out dif-
ferently . . . A lump formed in his throat, and he felt
sick with disappointment.

"Kemo Sabe?" Tonto said gently.

"Yes?"

"You can go to her. Take the mask off forever."

He looked at the Indian and felt almost ashamed for
his momentary weakness. He'd given his promise—to
Dan, to Tonto, and to the People. This was his blood
brother and their trails would never cross nor grow
apart.

"Goodbye, Amy."

"Who is she?"

"Someone I rode a stage with a long, long time ago,"
he whispered as she disappeared around a corner.
"Come on, I see the cantina up ahead."

The cantina was empty at this hour, except for the
bartender and a lonely drinker at the last table. The
Lone Ranger moved to the figure he recognized as the
betrayer, Collins. For one moment, he struggled to
keep from grabbing the traitor by the neck and stran-
gling him to death.

But he gained control, because he wanted Cavendish. Cavendish was the man who'd stood upon the
edge of the cliff and shot Dan twice in the chest. His
eyes now gazed through that same pair of bullet holes.

"Collins!" he said, settling into a chair across from this hated man.

The betrayer blinked owlishly. In drunken jest, he raised his hands and giggled. "You're too late, mister. I already been held up once. The bar dog got all my money."

"You were at Bryant's Gap."

The hands came down. The slack grin died. "No secret."

"Tell me about that day."

Collins leaned back in his chair and squinted his eys, trying to focus clearly.

"Where's Cavendish?"

"How would I know?"

"Because you led those Texas Rangers to him. Now —lead me!"

Collins poured another drink, spilling it all over the table. He swallowed it in a gulp. "You have it all wrong, mister. I'm a damned hero!"

"You're damned, all right," the Lone Ranger grated.

Collins recoiled in shock. "You're crazy! I don't know Cavendish! I don't know what the hell you're talking about."

"Yes, you do."

Collins grabbed the whiskey bottle, but the Lone Ranger's hand closed like a steel trap on his wrist. "For the last time! Where's Cavendish? How many followers does he have? Why did you set up the Texas Rangers that day? Tell me! It's your only salvation!"

Collins' eyes were wide and glassy with fear. "Train," he breathed. "Cavendish wants the train!"

"What train? Why does . . ."

The booming rifle threw Collins face down across the table with a hole in his back. As the Lone Ranger pushed away and reached for his guns, he saw something that made him freeze, then run for escape. Sheriff Justin A. Wiatt had fired the gun—fired with Tonto as his shield.

"Damn!" Wiatt screamed toward his deputy. He

jumped out the rear door. "Get him, boy! Gun him down in the alley!"

Heat waves shimmered off the land, and the people of Del Rio were hot and angry as the stranger named Wald spat in the dust and prodded the sweaty crowd. "Collins was a hero. The only survivor. Then he gets back-shot! It ain't right."

"Hell, no, it ain't," someone answered bitterly. "He deserved better after the hell he survived in that canyon."

"That stinkin' Indian never even let him see the bullet coming. Collins never had a chance!"

Wald raised a hangman's noose and shook it like a bullfighter's red cape. "I'm tellin' you folks that we don't owe that Indian any better than Collins got. A trial is too civilized for that savage!"

"You're right, Wald. I say we give him the same chance he gave Collins. String him up—now!"

Wald shook the rope at the sky, and the crowd roared, then surged toward Justin A. Wiatt's office.

The deputy pushed the window shade back and turned toward his boss. "Just like you said, Wald got 'em stirred up and they're a' comin'!"

Wiatt took a peek and saw Cavendish's man leading them forward. He looked around at Tonto. "Hey, Crazy Horse! Kiss this earth goodbye, 'cause you're about to depart for the happy hunting grounds."

Then the two men began to laugh, and they couldn't stop until the banging at the front door grew very loud.

The sheriff composed his face and headed outside. "Okay, hold it, all of you! What's going on here?"

Wald lifted the noose in one fist and pointed his gun at the sheriff with the other. "Don't get in the way," he warned meanly. "We're takin' the Indian! Step aside."

The sheriff had no intention of doing anything else. "All right," he said grudgingly. "Me and the deputy can't buck the whole town. Go on ahead and string him up. Just don't break up my office getting him outa here. He's a fighter, by damned, and you'd better all rush him at once or he'll tear your heads off!"

Seven of the mob rushed past him and into the jail cell. There was a loud scuffling inside. Several angry cries were emitted before they dragged Tonto into the street. His arms were pinned and one eyebrow was cut and bleeding. A big man spat in his face and punched him square in the mouth, splitting both lips. Tonto's head rocked back and he sagged for a moment before they lifted him up.

The crowd roared its approval as they dragged Tonto down the street toward Del Rio's gallows. When they reached the gallows steps they shoved him up to the platform.

"Let's see how far that red neck of his will stretch!"

A bottle of whiskey glinted as it was upended in the sunlight. "He's gonna do the strangulation jig! Wahoo!"

They slapped the noose over Tonto's head and jerked it tight around his neck.

Now that it was all ready to be done, the onlookers grew silent, maybe thinking about how their own times would come—one way or another. Some swallowed as though their throats were suddenly very dry. Others fidgeted uncomfortably, studying their dusty boots, their dirt-creased finger joints.

"You got anything to say before we pull the rope?" Wald yelled. "Can you understand English, you filthy redskin?"

Tonto understood. Through the beatings he'd taken since being led away from the cantina the night before, he'd heard nothing but viciousness and lies. But not once had he spoken nor would he ever again, because he meant to die like a warrior—with great courage and dignity.

"This is for Collins," snarled the hangman as he gripped the trap-door handle.

The handle splintered into a thousand pieces and,

appearing from around the street corner, the great white stallion raced straight into the crowd.

"Come on, Silver!" cried the Lone Ranger with both guns blazing.

Sheriff Wiatt drew his own pistol and then screamed in pain as it exploded in his fist.

"Kemo Sabe!"

Someone lunged for the bullet-splintered trap-door handle and, just as he fell on it, a silver bullet cut the hangman's rope.

As the rope broke, Tonto took a flying jump toward the mighty stallion. He landed perfectly. As Silver charged down the main street of Del Rio, a single cry echoed through the town and floated on the dust. They all heard it. It was a sound to be remembered.

"Hi yo, Silver!"

Chapter 12

THE Lone Ranger poked at the campfire. There were many things on his mind and foremost among them was Butch Cavendish.

"Tonto, are you certain?"

The Indian nodded. "Yes. I heard them last night after I was beaten and lying on the cell floor. Wiatt and his deputy work for Cavendish. They spoke of Buffalo Bill Cody, General Custer, and Wild Bill Hickok. The sheriff said Cavendish will fight them and win."

The Lone Ranger's eyes stared into the flames. "He's smart. Tonto, there has to be a reason. I must find out why he would fight *them!*"

Butch Cavendish stood before the huge table and inspected the scale model. Every inch of terrain along a twenty-mile section of railroadbed had been exactly reproduced. Hills, cliffs, gorges, and even trees made the replica as fine as anyone could hope to produce.

"Roll the train," Cavendish ordered, slapping a military pointer against his freshly pressed trousers.

One of his aides began to push the miniature train and Cavendish's pointer rose to tap once upon each car. "Coal tender, horses transport, troops' car, club or smoking car and, here, gentlemen, is the last and the one in which we are most interested—the presidential car!"

He looked at each of them as the aide kept pushing the little train along its tracks. "Listen sharply, my friends, for there will be no mistakes during this operation. Failure to carry out your orders will result in the same punishment as Gattlin and Stillwell received."

He smiled at them. "Is that understood perfectly?"

"Yes, sir!" they snapped.

"Very good." He turned his attention to the miniature panorama spread across the table before them. "Now, here is the water tower. On top, we see a pair of soldiers. They are Whitliff and Richardson."

"Yes, sir!"

"Now, gentlemen, after taking on water, the train begins to climb toward the summit on exactly the grade we've constructed here for your examination. Westlake, I want you positioned here."

"Yes, sir!"

"The train will be laboring toward this tunnel." He rapped the pointer down hard. "Eastman, Neeley. You will be here."

The aide propelled the train into the tunnel. Butch Cavendish smiled with devilish delight. Then he shoved the pointer in between the club car and that of the United States president. The little clasp between them broke and the presidential car came loose and hurtled back down the grade by itself. It flew off the table and crashed against the wall.

Cavendish laughed at the aide's stricken expression, then addressed those who watched him.

"Gentleman, you have just witnessed a runaway railroad car hurtling alone down the tracks. If your intelligence permits, try to imagine a single man alone in that car—imagine he is the president of the United States."

"But, Major Cavendish!" a lieutenant blurted, "you said we were going to take Grant hostage."

"I did?" His eyebrows rose in mock surprise. "Oh, yes. You are correct, Perlmutter. Then I guess I'd better tell you the rest of my plan."

Exactly an hour later, Butch Cavendish swaggered out to inspect the army of horsemen who awaited his command. Each mounted rider held his animal under tight rein, and the formation looked very professional.

"Well done," he said, feeling the excitement building inside. Here was his army—his means of accomplishing the impossible dream.

"Perlmutter?"

"Yes, Major?"

"Have you and the other officers made your inspection?"

"Yes, sir. All troops properly armed and militarily attired. Equipment in good working order."

"Excellent!" Cavendish replied, as his black stallion was led forward. "Troops, we are ready to begin one of the most brilliant and daring military coups of all time. If everyone does his part, we cannot fail to change the course of history."

He paused for effect. *"But,* if even one of you makes an error, the mission will surely end in defeat. And I promise that such an error will be fatal."

Cavendish knew damned well there would be no mistakes. There hadn't been a single one at Bryant's Gap and there wouldn't be one now. This was a military force such as he'd always dreamed of commanding.

He strode to his waiting horse. "Texas for Texans!" he cried. "Tomorrow we will make her our own!"

As he wheeled the prancing stallion, the troops moved in smartly behind.

Butch Cavendish rode alone at the head of his army.

If they could have seen his face, they'd have been astounded to know that he could smile.

Amy Striker rushed out of her newspaper office and peered down the street. She was late. The crowd had already gathered before the town hall steps. These days, she was always late. Too much to do alone. Her eyes were dark with fatigue and her hands ink-stained and battered from the hard work of operating the old Gutenberg printing press. Someday, she vowed, locking her office, she'd . . .

"Miss Striker. Oh, Miss Striker!" The little boy stood panting for air. "I've got a message for you from the padre. He wants to see you in church. Right away!"

Amy frowned. "Father Monteleone?"

"Uh-uh, another padre."

"Can't it wait? I'm late for the meeting."

"No," Tom said stubbornly. "The padre said it was *very* important you come right now. I *promised* I'd bring you."

As she hurried toward the small Catholic church, the boy yelled, "Gosh, Miss Striker. You musta done something *real* bad."

Amy entered the old Spanish church made of crumbling adobe and felt its cool peacefulness. Up near the altar, she observed several old Mexican women bent in prayer, lit by the green and red shafts of light from the stained-glass windows. Amy moved past a wooden statue of Saint Joseph, to where a hooded priest knelt in prayer before a lovely gold-painted statue of Saint Mary.

It was very dark in the church and her eyes were not yet accustomed to the light, but the man before her was unmistakably the new padre. "You sent for me, Father?"

In a beautiful Spanish accent, he answered without turning from the Virgin Mary to whom he prayed.

"Yes, my child. You cause me great worry."

128

Amy frowned. "I don't understand. I have committed no sin."

"Of course not. The matter concerns your newspaper writings. They are very brave . . . yet very dangerous."

"Father. Would you have me print lies?"

"No!" His voice seemed to have changed, but Amy shook it off as a trick of acoustics.

Another padre with two parishioners approached. Quickly, Amy's padre said, "Please, in here . . ." He ushered her into the confessional and took his place on the other side of the partition.

He cleared his throat. "No," he whispered calmly. "Yet I pray that you act with prudence. What I now have to say concerns another man who is your friend and will protect you against the murderers of your uncle."

"Butch Cavendish had my Uncle Lucas silenced. Everyone knows that. And John, dear John, was also murdered trying to bring Cavendish to justice. The Texas Rangers were lured into an ambush!"

Amy fought to regain her composure. "I am sorry, Father. I lost two men I loved."

There was a vast silence, and when the padre spoke, it seemed to be with great difficulty. "I came to tell you about this man who will help you always. You will recognize him because he wears a mask."

"A mask?"

"Yes, Amy, but it is not for reasons of evil doing. He is dedicated to law and order. He asked me to tell you that he will not rest until he has brought Cavendish to justice."

Amy couldn't hide her skepticism. "Thank you, Father. But until this mysterious masked benefactor actually gets Cavendish, I'll keep writing in hopes of stirring up the public's conscience."

"You mustn't! You'll get hurt!"

"I'm *already* hurt, Father. Inside I hurt everywhere because of Cavendish. You, of all people, must understand pain, because you deal with it always. Thank you for your concern, Padre. You see, I cannot stop writing. It's all I have."

"I understand," he whispered sadly.

"Now, Father, with all due respect, you must excuse me. I'm on my way to a meeting for President Grant's arrival."

"The president! Coming here?" His voice was urgent.

Puzzled, Amy responded, "Why, yes, on the afternoon train."

"Today?"

"I think the children are more excited about seeing Buffalo Bill and—"

"My God . . ."

"What's wrong, Father?" Amy half-rose from the confessional bench.

From behind the partition, the padre muttered, "You should have gone to San Francisco."

"What?" Amy's hand flew out and touched the barrier between them. "Father, how . . ."

He whispered urgently, "I must go!"

"But, Father. This masked man, who . . ."

"Trust him," the padre answered. "Goodbye, my dear. Remember, he also loves you!"

"Who? Father . . ." There was no answer. "Father?"

Amy stepped out of the confessional. The church was empty. She opened the padre's side of the confessional. It, too, was empty, except for a shiny object on the bench . . . a silver bullet.

The Lone Ranger joined Tonto behind the livery barn, where he held Silver and Scout ready.

"I have the answer, Tonto," the Lone Ranger declared. "Just before Collins died in the cantina, I asked him why Cavendish found it necessary to slaughter my brother and the Texas Rangers."

"What was his answer, Kemo Sabe?"

" 'Train.' Cavendish wants the train!" The Lone

Ranger peered across the horses at Tonto. "That's got to be it! Hickok, Cody, and Custer are on it with Ulysses Grant. Butch Cavendish plans to attack our United States President!"

"Maybe," the Indian said quietly, "it would be best for my people if he succeeds."

"What?"

"Your Great White Father in Washington does *nothing* for the Indian!" Tonto swore in an outburst of fury. "He has allowed the whites to take our lands, conquer and kill our people. Treaties mean nothing to your President Ulysses Grant."

"Tonto, that's not true."

"It *is* true, Kemo Sabe. You saw the People. They are starving. Like caged animals, they wait for their white masters to throw them a crust of bread when, once, they had buffalo meat. The whites will never live up to their treaties. They hate the red man and will not rest until our bones bleach in the sun!"

The Lone Ranger gazed deep into his friend's eyes and saw the pain and anger. He didn't try to argue because he knew the Indian spoke the truth. "Maybe we can change things, Tonto."

Tonto shook his head. "Too many times has the Indian lived on promises, only to taste burnt ashes. I guard myself against yet another false hope."

He stood up. "I need to walk in the darkness, for my Spirit is heavy when I think of what was said and done to me here in Del Rio."

"Tonto . . . ?"

The Indian held up his hand and the Lone Ranger remained silent. "Kemo Sabe. You are my blood brother and have saved my life twice—once as a boy, today as a man."

"I would have died at Bryant's Gap if you hadn't saved mine," the Lone Ranger quietly reminded him.

"Yes. Always it will be this way between us. But hear me well, Kemo Sabe. I trust you alone."

The Lone Ranger understood very well. In those

brief moments when he'd opened fire on those about to hang his Indian friend, he'd seen naked hatred in the eyes of the mob. Maybe if they saved the president of the United States, things could change and Tonto's people and all Indians would benefit. The Lone Ranger's thoughts about the injustices the Indians had endured switched to Butch Cavendish. He had terrorized his own people too long. Things *would* change if he and Tonto lived to make them better.

Change must begin with Cavendish. But he and Tonto would need help.

Chapter 13

Amy Striker's thoughts were troubled as she left the church. Who was that padre? And why would a masked man try to befriend her? It was all so mysterious and, if she hadn't heard the words from a priest, she'd have discounted them entirely. But now, as she approached the town hall steps, she realized there were other, more immediate problems to be faced.

"Mrs. Vogelsang," the mayor called, "could I have your attention, ladies?" The clattering voices quieted. "Thank you! How is the ladies' auxiliary coming along with refreshments?"

Mrs. Vogelsang, a large woman with an officious manner, announced, "I have everything under control. Mrs. Galloway is baking our American flag cake, and we are going to have twenty-two gallons of chocolate ice cream."

The mayor blinked the sweat out of his eyes and mopped his face. "Wonderful!" he exclaimed. "Just how are you going to keep it from melting way out on the prairie?"

Mrs. Vogelsang's mouth fell open. "Why . . . why . . ." She turned to the woman at her side. "Gretchen, why didn't *you* think of that?"

"Me? Why didn't you?"

"How should I know?" came the angry retort. "I'm not in charge of ice cream. My department is fireworks!"

"Ladies. Ladies," the mayor yelled. "Please, we must get on with the arrangements!"

"Ladies!" Amy was exasperated. "We haven't got time for this bickering among ourselves. President Grant's train is now on its way to Del Rio!"

"It's fine for you to talk, Miss Striker. *You* don't have twenty-two gallons of chocolate mush to worry about! In fact, unless I'm totally mistaken, you haven't *anything* to worry about since you're not on a single one of our welcoming committees."

Amy's face reddened. "Mrs. Vogelsang, I'm working night and day readying Del Rio's petitions to get federal help so that Butch Cavendish is run down and brought to trial. Furthermore, when all the ice cream, fireworks, and cookies are gone, those petitions will still be in our president's hands as a constant reminder of just what kind of terror we're facing here on the border."

"*Well*, Miss Striker. That is all very fine, except that President Grant would be ill disposed toward our petitions—to say the least—if he left our party hungry or with indigestion, and I'm . . ."

"Ladies! Gentlemen!"

The ladies' auxiliary shrieked in unison at the sight of the tall, masked man. Amy remembered the padre's words and moved closer.

The Lone Ranger held up his hands. "May I have your attention, please? I don't wish to intrude, yet you must listen to what I have to say."

"Why should we?" the mayor challenged. "I'm not accustomed to dealing with masked men or Indians. What's behind that mask?"

Before the Lone Ranger could answer, another citizen yelled, "Say, wasn't the redskin that killed Eddie Collins saved by a masked man?"

"Yeah!" another answered. "Is there a reward?"

"Gotta be! Sheriff Wiatt . . ."

The Lone Ranger curbed his mounting irritation. "All right!" he shouted, "I admit I'm the one who rescued Tonto. But he didn't kill Collins—Sheriff Wiatt did."

"What the hell you talking about!" the mayor raved. "We've a fine sheriff and you're the ones who're guilty."

"If we were guilty," the Lone Ranger said evenly, "we wouldn't have come back to save President Grant's life. And to do it—we need your help."

The crowd stirred restlessly, then a voice demanded, "What's Collins' death got to do with the president's life?"

"Everything," the Lone Ranger said bluntly. "Butch Cavendish didn't want Collins to tell me that he's planning to intercept President Grant's train. We need your help to stop him from carrying out those plans."

The mayor examined the faces of his voters. He decided it was time to assume control. "Now just a minute, stranger. You and your friend are under real suspicion in the matter of Collins being shot. And now you have the nerve to walk in here and make these preposterous charges that—first—our Sheriff Wiatt murdered Collins and—second—that the presidential car is going to be attacked by Butch Cavendish."

His eyebrows cocked up questioningly. "Just how far are you willing to stretch your credibility and our imaginations?"

"You must believe me," the Lone Ranger insisted, knowing he wasn't going to get their help and unable to figure a way to prove his story. "We can't afford to stand here wasting our time arguing."

"Mister, do you and your injun friend know who else is on that train? Well, before you go off the deep end of the dam, let me tell you. In addition to a whole troop of United States cavalry, he's got the protection of George A. Custer, Wild Bill Hickok, and Buffalo Bill Cody! And that's enough protection for anybody."

The Lone Ranger looked at Tonto, then back at the crowd. "Is it? Butch Cavendish trapped twelve of the best men in Texas over at Bryant's Gap. No one except Tonto and I know how—but he did. And, one way or another, he'll figure out a way to trap the president of this country unless you folks take action."

"We're trying to," Mrs. Vogelsang crabbed, "and right now we're tryin' to figure how to keep twenty-two gallons of chocolate ice cream frozen!"

Tonto's eyes rolled upward in disgust, but he held his tongue.

"Yeah," the man named Sherman echoed. "And you're never sure but what those damned Mexican fireworks won't blow your fingers off! And anyway, how do we know you're not one of Cavendish's men trying to set us all up and ruin the celebration altogether?"

Amy Striker had stood about all she could of this pettiness. "I don't understand you people!" she cried. "Can't you hear what this man is saying? There's going to be an attack on the president's life and we're the *only* ones who can stop it."

When no one offered to help, she walked up to the Lone Ranger. "I'll ride with you."

It was the kind of simple, unaffected gesture he knew he could expect from this woman. He should have been prepared for it. Yet it still moved the Lone Ranger deeply.

"Thank you, Miss Striker. But . . . well, ma'am, I can't accept your offer—not against Butch Cavendish's army, I can't."

The men in the crowd shifted uncomfortably and, one by one, offered their excuses.

"I, uh . . . I got a wife and kids."

"Lookee here, Miss Amy, I believe in law and or-

der as much as the next man, but I ain't getting paid
to uphold it. Where's our sheriff? This kind of thing is
what we're supposed to be paying him for."

"He's right," another groused. "Besides, with Cody
and Hickok there, we'd just get in the way. Anyway,
my wife needs looking after. She's got a headache
today."

Amy turned toward the masked man to try to apol-
ogize for the cowards of Del Rio. "Mister . . ."

The tall masked man and his Indian friend were
gone.

Amy bit her lip and spoke to the crowd. "If what
he told us was the truth, then we're going to be solely
responsible for whatever happens to the president of
the United States of America. And no one can say we
were not warned."

She left them at the town hall steps, and before
she was out of hearing, Mrs. Vogelsang was asking
for a show of hands on whether they ought to make
oatmeal or gingersnap cookies.

The opulent smoking car rolled west toward Del
Rio beside the Rio Grande. James B. Hickok, or Wild
Bill, as he preferred, was enjoying this public-relations
jaunt. Without a doubt, this was what high living was
all about. He'd served through some rough years as a
stagecoach driver, town marshal, and a bull whacker
on the Santa Fe Trail. During the Civil War, he'd been
a federal scout and a guerrilla fighter. Later, he'd
scouted for his old friend and member of this entourage—Lieutenant Colonel George A. Custer.

But now he was rollin' high, wide, and handsome.
The chair he sat in was of fine leather; a long, richly
polished mahogany bar was close at hand and well
stocked to his liking. And, if he wanted to display his
shooting ability—well, he could do that, too, for the
chairs swiveled for gunning antelope, buffalo, or whatever else moved out on the plains. Hell, there was even
a bunch of fancy high-powered hunting rifles hanging

on the walls, along with those blasted stuffed animal heads.

Wild Bill didn't cotton to having a grizzly's mouth hanging over his head as he dealt the cards. But he guessed he'd keep quiet since he was winning.

"I'm out," Custer said, throwing down his hand in disgust.

"Shoulda seen it a 'comin'," Buffalo Bill drawled. "Man's got to learn how to cut his losses."

"That's right," Wild Bill chuckled, eyeing the Mexican general who was wearing about three pounds of medals and ribbons on his chubby chest. Still, General Aurillio Rodriguez was a fine poker player and not to be underestimated.

"General? As you can see, I've an ace, a queen, and a four with two more cards to go."

"Not nearly good enough to beat my pair of aces and the nine," Rodriguez answered. He peeked once more at his hole cards. "I bet two hundred more, Señor 'Eecock."

Wild Bill tugged at his moustache. He glanced at Cody and Custer. Hellfire, he thought, staring at the big pot. This is the best stakes yet. Can't quit now.

"Two hundred, general, and I'll raise you another two."

Rodriguez smiled as though he couldn't be more pleased, and that made Hickok squirm a mite. Perhaps the fat little general was bluffing but, if so, he was mighty good at it.

"I see you, Wild Beel, and I raise you—one thousand dollars."

Holy buffalo chips! Wild Bill grinned away his panic. What in blazes had he got besides the aces and nine? "Cody, lend me three hundred."

Buffalo Bill stretched indolently and reached inside his fringed jacket. He pulled out a wad of money and counted it slowly. "Hickok, you best know what you're doin' this time."

He took a deep breath and pushed the money forward. "Call, Aurillio."

The General flipped the two hole cards face up. An ace of spades and a six.

"Three aces, señor." His hand reached for the stack of poker chips.

"Wait a minute, General! What's high?"

Aurillio Rodriguez was no longer smiling. "Three aces, nine high, señor."

"Not good enough," Wild Bill drawled, turning his two hole cards up. Everyone gasped at the ace of spades and ace of hearts. The general's eyes swept back and forth between his own ace of spades and Hickok's, as the big man reached for the money. "No sir, General. Almost, but not quite. I've also got three aces, queen high. Sorry. You lose."

"Interesting hand," Custer said dryly.

"For certain," Buffalo Bill observed. "Ain't seen many like that before."

General Rodriguez threw out his hands in an appeal for fairness. "But, gentlemen, you cannot do thees!"

Wild Bill cradled the pot and shrugged helplessly. "Well, Generalissimo, it's your play now. What's it going to be?"

The game was as clear as the Texas air, and Aurillio Rodriguez had not become a general either by lack of brains or courage; he knew when he was up against a stacked deck.

He forced a laugh. "That was very good, my gringo friends! Well done! Perhaps next time, we play poker in Mexico. Yes?"

Hickok shoved the money into his leather bag after returning Buffalo Bill's three hundred plus a hefty amount of interest. "General, I'll play poker in Mexico."

"Bueno, señor. I knew you were a sporting gringo. When?"

"The day hell freezes over, amigo. Adios, now," he

said, tipping his hat and moving toward the presidential car with Custer and Cody.

If the club car was richly appointed, the president's car was downright elegant. The walls were draped with red velvet, and the fittings were of polished silver to match the crystal. A silver chandelier hung tinkling over the desk where President Ulysses Grant hunched, writing a speech.

"Gentlemen!" he called, relieved by the interruption. "How did the cards fall? You are upholding our southern diplomatic relations, aren't you?"

"You'd have been proud of us, Mister President," Custer said gravely. "And I'm pleased to report that Mexico has just made another wise concession."

President Grant knew better than to press the unanswered question. "Listen up, gentlemen. I want you to hear this damned speech I've been writing while you boys were fleecing poor Aurillio."

He cleared his throat and began reading. "Ladies and gentlemen, today I'm here to say that our great nation has been torn long enough by war and dissension. It is the policy of this government to facilitate peaceful negotiations whenever possible with our more honorable red brothers. However, we will not tolerate or stand aside while outrageous acts of barbarous nature are committed on the American plains by marauding Indians. And so, ladies and gentlemen, I'm here to say that, as your president, I will use all my power to defend your lives no matter what the cost."

Hickok dared to clap and yelled, "Damn good! I'd vote for you, Mister President!"

But George A. Custer wasn't smiling at all. "It's a tough speech and one long overdue, sir. Like the buffalo, the Indian needs to be controlled. There are just too damn many of them. Either we eliminate some or maintain 'em as a species of blood-suckin' paupers."

Grant's eyes grew distant. "I don't know the answer," he admitted. "Only time will tell what's going to happen to the red man. Probably, he'll go the way of his livelihood, the buffalo."

His big fists clenched. "But, until then, I mean to stop the murdering—and I'll do it!"

The water tower looked exactly like the tiny replica in his office, as Butch Cavendish and his men galloped down alongside the railroad tracks. Ahead, and past the tower, he saw the shining rails begin their ascent toward the summit beyond.

Cavendish wasted no words but motioned part of his force on toward the summit while he and the rest halted beside the tower.

"Dismount and put the horses and wagons under cover. Perlmutter?"

"Yes, sir!"

"Get the men in position at once. I will ride by in three minutes. Anyone in sight will be severely punished."

"Yes, sir!"

Three minutes later, Butch Cavendish snapped his gold pocket watch shut and began his tour. He was the only moving thing in that entire panorama. Richardson and Whitliff were on top of the water tower and completely undetectable from anywhere but the sky.

Cavendish reined his horse down the rails toward where the train would soon be coming. He studied the draw intently and saw nothing that would indicate that fifty mounted riders sat in wait nearby.

The leader dismounted the black horse and squatted down beside the tracks. He carefully balanced a matchstick across the steel rails, knowing that it would vibrate, then fall, long before his own eyes or ears could detect the oncoming train. It was a trick he'd used in the war to derail more than one troop train in Dixieland.

Two hours passed and the fifty mounted riders sweated in the tight confinement of the draw. Richardson and Whitliff grew dizzy on the water tower, watching heat waves shimmer across the earth.

But nothing moved.

Nothing, that is, until the match began to vibrate. Slowly, then faster, until it danced off the shining steel rails.

Butch Cavendish rose to his feet and grinned. Yeah! Just like playing war all over again.

Only this time, instead of a bunch of poor Confederate soldiers, he'd be taking the president of the United States!

Chapter 14

BUFFALO Bill Cody handled the fancy gold-plated rifle as if it were an extension of himself. In one quick movement, he leveled a shell into the chamber and fired out the car window. He watched the rabbit go down, kicking circles in the dirt as the train swept by.

"Damn fine rifle," he commented. "But not as fine as Lucrezia Borgia."

General Rodriguez lifted his eyebrows questioningly.

"His Springfield Model '65," Hickok drawled. "A .58 caliber converted from a muzzle-loader used in the Civil War so it could take cartridges. Fella named Allin sawed off the end of the barrel so you could slip in a bullet. They ain't very pretty but hard to beat for accuracy."

"Thank you, señor." He turned to Buffalo Bill. "What is the most dangerous animal you have encountered on your hunts Mr. Cody?"

"That's easy enough. Grizzly, for sure. Once, I shot

one right through the heart with my Springfield, but it just kept a 'comin' like this here train. He was dead as hell but his mind was made up to take me with him."

The Mexican's eyes widened. "Then how did you stop this greezzlie?"

"Didn't. I threw him the damned gun and told him to reload and take his best shot at my backside!"

Hickok and Custer roared with laughter and the general tentatively joined them.

"You play leetle joke," he scolded after the three frontiersmen regained their composure. "But eez no joke to me. I think the most dangerous prey is the wild boar."

"You mean a pig?" Hickok blurted. "Hellfire, Mister Rodriguez, them tusky little devils can't move near as fast as a mountain lion dropping outa a tree. You ever wound a big cat in heavy forest without dogs, you'd better walk light and keep your finger on a hair trigger."

"You're all wrong," George A. Custer told them seriously. "The most dangerous animal—by far—is *man*."

Butch Cavendish knelt behind the brush cover that had been piled up for his concealment. His eyes never left the train as it neared the water tower. Already, it was going much slower because of the steep grade as the trail approached the summit.

Now, as the locomotive belched and smoked, Cavendish saw his two men on the tower lower the water chute and jump into it. For one heart-stopping moment, the chute dangled out into space, then Whitliff leaped out onto the top of the horse car. He struck the roof hard and almost lost his balance before he grabbed hold and waved.

Richardson did it better, maybe because he'd had a chance to observe his partner's mistake. Whatever the reason, he acted like a kid going over a millrace and enjoying every inch of the ride as he hurtled down to land on the soldiers' car.

Cavendish let out a huge sigh of relief as the train huffed by, and he saw Richardson scramble to the rear of the troop car and aim his rifle down to cover the exit. At the same time, Whitliff crawled across the horse-car roof until he stood up and leapt to the coal tender. Now he, too, aimed his rifle from a hidden position onto the unsuspecting engineer and fireman.

"Well done!" Cavendish exclaimed. "Perfect execution!"

The train was puffing to the top of the hill. Westlake silently dropped to the club car, then tiptoed across the swaying roof and vaulted onto the last car—that of the president. He took a kneeling position with his rifle trained on the car doors below.

As they slowly approached the summit, a lookout slipped from his hiding place and fired a flare to signal the major that all was going as planned.

In the club car, the president and his entourage were enjoying a sumptuous lunch served on crystal and china by two identical waiters. They were just about to finish when the president's secretary glanced at his watch. "Oh, dear, sir! I'm afraid we're soon due for a stop. A place called Del Rio."

"Another delay? I could walk as fast as we're traveling now."

The secretary smiled tepidly. "We're almost to the summit, Mister President. Apparently Del Rio isn't far beyond and they *are* expecting you to eat a cake or something. It's a celebration. At least, that's what this memo says."

"Damn!" the President shouted, waving his greasy napkin. "I've just eaten. Besides, I don't want any cake and it's too hot for me to add to the temperature." He glared at the bearer of this news. "Get word to the engineer that we'll be stopping, but for just three minutes. No more! Not one breath more!"

"Yes, Mister President."

"And next time consult your notes *before* I've had lunch!"

"Yes, Mister President."

Grant glared at the departing figure. "I should fire him for incompetence. Cake, indeed!"

He threw down his napkin and stood looking at Buffalo Bill and Custer. "You fellas do yourselves a big favor and stay the hell out of politics. Hear, now?"

When they nodded, Grant headed for the rear door. "I better practice that speech for the good voters of Del Rio. I don't want to be disturbed until we get there. Please tell that to my incompetent secretary."

The train chugged through a bend set in a narrow gorge and aimed for the summit tunnel up ahead. From either side of the gorge, Eastman and Neeley jumped onto the club car, signaled to the waiting trio, and edged to the gap between the last two cars.

Everything was going perfectly.

The locomotive belched into the tunnel, and Eastman and Neeley dropped between the cars. While Eastman waited with drawn guns, his partner's fingers located the pin and yanked it loose.

The presidential car broke free, came to a gentle stop, then began to inch backwards. It picked up speed for fifty yards and burst out of the tunnel into daylight. Another hundred yards and it lurched around a sharp bend and gunned into a straightaway. It was really rolling now!

President Ulysses Grant dropped his quill pen and did a double take out the window.

"What the . . . we're going backwards! Hickok! Cody! What the hell is . . ."

The words died in his throat as the president threw open the door and gaped at an empty track. He was alone. The train was gone! The tunnel a vanishing dot in the mountainside.

Grant staggered back into his car and poured a drink as the landscape blurred across his window. He figured he was going to die and he might as well go with some first-class whiskey in his belly.

Cavendish had seen the signaling flare and knew there were only moments left before the presidential car would come swooping around the last curve and burst into the straightaway directly above. If they weren't ready, the party would be all over.

"Take your positions!" he cried.

The presidential car hurtled into view and swept down toward them like an avenging angel. Cavendish swung onto his horse and sank his spurs as the animal clawed its way up the hillside. He reached his vantage point and reined his mount around. He studied the onrushing car as it flashed into the straightaway with its presidential banners and flags waving madly. Then it blazed toward the water tower.

"Come on!" he whispered. "Not so fast! Not so fast, damn you!"

Westlake made his move, jumped to the platform, and applied all his strength to the emergency brake. At the last possible moment, the car came to a screeching halt and was instantly surrounded by Cavendish's men.

"Magnificent!" Cavendish congratulated himself. He nudged his horse forward and rode down to see if the president of the United States was dead or alive.

President Grant was very much alive. For a long moment, he lay sprawled on the floor of the car wondering *why* he'd survived. At the speed the car had been traveling, he had no right at all to be counted among the living. He patted himself to be certain he hadn't died and gone to heaven or hell.

Deciding that he was intact, the president righted himself and stood shakily. He peered out the window and saw the band of armed men who surrounded him.

Not so astonishing after all, he concluded sadly, as the picture began to fall into place.

"President Grant! Are you alive in there?" boomed

a voice. "If so, come on out before I send in my troops!"

Ulysses Grant scowled. Then he tucked in his shirt, brushed his coat, picked up his hat from the floor, and headed for the door.

The sun nearly blinded him as he stepped outside. Its golden glare haloed Butch Cavendish as Grant studied the figure.

"I am Major Bartholomew Cavendish," the glowering rider proclaimed. "And you, Mister President, are my prisoner."

Grant shaded his eyes and longed for the bottle of whiskey he'd dropped when he'd struck the floor. He tried to force bravado into his voice. "Are you mad? Do you have any idea what you are doing? You are threatening the president of the United States!"

Cavendish laughed outright and it sent chills up Grant's spine. "Mister Cavendish, I demand an explanation for this outrageous conduct."

The laughter died as though sabre-slashed. "You demand nothing! Until I say so, you are my property. Step down and come forth!"

"Go to hell," Grant rumbled.

Cavendish motioned to his lieutenants, and Grant decided that they were too dangerous to challenge. He swallowed his outrage and considerable pride and descended from the presidential car.

"Where are we going, Cavendish?"

"*Major* Cavendish," the voice corrected.

"Very well." Then it hit him in the face like a closed fist. Major Butch Cavendish! Union army! Missionary Ridge and Vicksburg. A court-martial for rape and murder! Dishonorable discharge.

"Ah," the voice purred. "I see you're finally remembering."

He nodded stiffly. "Yes," he gritted, through clenched teeth. "I remember you very well. It would appear you still haven't learned your lesson."

Cavendish smirked. "General, we both know I just got caught doing what you'd have liked to do."

Cavendish laughed heartily and gave his orders. "Bring up that extra horse. We're riding fast. And if it'll make you move any quicker, I am ordering a celebration in honor of a long-awaited reunion!"

The president was shoved toward his horse. Cavendish rode in beside him and hissed. "But *this* time, *I'll* be the judge and jury, Mister President. Your office will be on trial and the charge is treason and betrayal."

Two dirty men pitched the president headlong over the saddle, and the troopers' coarse laughter told Ulysses S. Grant what he'd already suspected—the verdict was in—guilty as charged!

Chapter 15

THE Lone Ranger and Tonto had no idea where Cavendish intended to strike.

"Tonto, we *must* follow these tracks to the southeast and hope we can reach the train before Cavendish."

He urged the white stallion onward, and the magnificent animal responded eagerly. As they galloped, the Lone Ranger's mind wrestled with doubts. Back in Del Rio, he'd almost weakened and revealed his true identity to Amy. In the future, he would guard himself more closely. Yet, when Amy had said she'd loved him . . .

The Lone Ranger forced his mind away from the woman he could never have and concentrated on the more immediate problem of stopping Cavendish.

"Kemo Sabe. Look!"

"The presidential train!" There was no mistaking the railroad car. American flags decorated the sides and banners hung from it everywhere. "We're too late, Tonto."

They dismounted and, while Tonto started reading hoofprints, the Lone Ranger scrambled over the railing and rushed inside.

"There are many horses, Kemo Sabe. Wagon horses unhitched and saddled—one for president."

"How can you tell?"

Tonto pointed out where the cinch rings had dragged across the dirt. Then he knelt close to the ground and showed the Lone Ranger the footprints of an unworn round-toed shoe. "This be your president, I think."

"Yes. I'm sure you're right." The masked man gathered up Silver's reins. "Tonto, we're too late, and now there is no choice but to ride into Butch Cavendish's stronghold. He'll be expecting company." The Lone Ranger studied his Indian friend closely.

"I read your troubled thoughts, Kemo Sabe. But, this time, it will be different. There is no betrayer among us and you have the silver bullets."

The Lone Ranger's hands brushed the twin gunbutts on his hips and his worries evaporated. "We'll find Cavendish," he promised, "and no matter how many troops stand between us and the president, a way *will* be found."

Then they vaulted into their saddles and raced along the still fresh trail leading eastward toward Cavendish's hideout.

It was late afternoon and, if Mrs. Vogelsang had brought her twenty-two gallons of ice cream, it would have been hot chocolate by now, Amy thought. Everything had been ready for hours. Lines of tables with once-clean linen had been set up. Now, the food was covered with dust and grit. A twenty-two-piece band of townsfolk was *still* rehearsing "Hail to the Chief," "The Star Spangled Banner," and the "Battle Hymn of the Republic"; the awful racket was getting on everyone's nerves.

Where was the presidential train? They'd been

telegraphed to expect it hours ago and, by now, the tedious and stiflingly hot hours had wilted the celebrants, their food, and the entire spirit of the occasion. Babies cried fitfully, kids bickered under the shade of the wagons, and even the horses stood hip shot and droopy-necked as they swatted flies with their tails.

Worst of all, the huge fifteen- by ten-foot American flag cake was melting.

But suddenly, they heard the miracle they'd all been praying for—a train whistle. *The train whistle!*

It was like an injection of energy. Everyone began yelling and dusting off the food and screaming at the kids to clean up, the president of these United States was coming! Only the band of Indians who'd stationed themselves off to one side of the festivities remained immobile and unimpressed.

In the few moments between the whistle blast and the train's steaming arrival, the carnival-like atmosphere of the Del Rio celebration had been revived and was in high gear. All the children took their places along the tracks and cheered as the train ground to a halt. The band leader waved his whittled-down broomstick and the musicians blew fresh sand and grit from their horns with the first notes of "Hail to the Chief," while their rivals, the Mexican mariachi players, blasted out their own raucous version of the same number. The cavalry soldiers stormed into rigid formation and began to execute precision drills in the tangled brush, photographers wrestled with their tripods and sweated under the black shrouds, hoping they'd get the right man and trying to remember what the president looked like.

In the heart of all but the stoic Indians, this was a big, *big* moment.

Wild Bill Hickok, General George Armstrong Custer, and Buffalo Bill Cody were the first ones to descend from the train, and the kids and young ladies went wild. After a few seconds, even the photographers could not resist those handsome smiling men

159

of destiny and clicked their shutters, then frantically began to reload.

George Custer's smile dwindled, then twisted into a mask of shock and horror.

"The president!" he gasped. "The president's car is missing!"

He swung on the presidential secretary. "Where is it? Where is he?"

The man paled. "I don't . . . don't know," he wheezed. "I think we . . . we lost them!"

"Shit!" Custer roared, leaping into the milling crowd and shoving them aside in his haste to reach the locomotive.

Amy Striker was a newspaper woman and she meant to get the full story immediately as she hurried after Custer. "General, the president's in trouble, isn't he?"

The man ignored her as he reached the locomotive. "Where did we lose it?" he stormed, loud enough to be heard over the huffing engine.

"I don't know, sir," the engineer wailed. "Last I saw it was when we were going up those switchbacks before the tunnel."

"Damnation, man! We're going back, after I get those two peacocks Hickok and Cody aboard. Put this train in reverse, and I want speed!"

"I'll give her all she can take," the brawny fireman promised as he grabbed his shovel.

"General," Amy persisted, as the man swiveled and strode back down the line. "I need to talk to you. I run the town's newspaper."

"Not a woman's business, ma'am."

"Maybe I can help!"

For the first time, the general actually looked at her. "Maybe you can, lady. Get a wire to Fort Davis. Tell them to send all the troops they've got down this line. And advise them I'm taking the ones I've got and riding after the president. Tell Fort Davis to hurry!"

Amy Striker was already in her buggy and applying

the whip, before the engine's big wheels spun into reverse and the train jolted backward to gather speed and puff off into the horizon. She remembered that the masked man had warned everyone that this was going to happen. Next time, maybe the good citizens of Del Rio would listen if any future president was foolish enough to re-enact this infamous day.

President Grant had studied the fortifications of this madman's stronghold and ruefully concluded that escape was impossible and that any attempt at a rescue would result in great losses.

"Impressive, aren't they?" Cavendish asked.

"What?"

Cavendish wiped his lips daintily with the napkin and took another sip of wine. "My military mementoes, of course. Ribbons and medals for valor, citations for bravery and, of course, that light cavalry sabre you're admiring."

Grant studied the sabre, though he'd seen plenty of them in battle. About thirty-two inches long, it was curved, with a graceful brass hilt. It was a good fighting weapon and very effective for close work during a cavalry charge.

"Where'd you get it?" Grant asked. "Off a fallen Southern officer?"

Cavendish flamed. "Damn you, man! How can you dare to insult me, when your own Washington fraternity is nothing but a stinkpot bubbling with vile corruption?"

Grant realized he'd come very close to triggering Cavendish's murderous urges. He could almost feel the finger of death tapping his shoulder and, though he was not afraid of dying, reason made him grow cautious. He strolled toward a massive pool table, selected and absently chalked a cue stick. With Cavendish's eyes still boring into him, Ulysses Grant made a perfect bank shot off the one-ball into the side pocket.

"How," Cavendish raged, "can the man that saved

161

the Union in war let it disintegrate into corruption during a time of peace?"

Grant eyed the number-two ball and decided he could just slice the angle and drop it in the corner pocket.

"Look around you, sir! Are you blind to the chaos and discontent that pervades this country?"

"I can't say as I've noticed," the president replied dryly, as he made his second successful shot in a row.

Cavendish slammed his fist down on the table, making the wine glasses jump a foot in the air. "Damn you, Mister President! If you can't see what the rest of the country's doing, perhaps you *will* notice *my* country: The Republic of New Texas!"

"What?" The cue stick fell from his hands and rolled across the felt-covered slate.

"You heard me," Cavendish grinned maliciously. "And please be assured that my necessary intervention will impair only slightly the so-called manifest destiny of these United States."

With trembling fingers, Grant retrieved his cue. "Cavendish, you're a diseased sonovabitch."

Then, ignoring the strangled, choking sound, followed by a tortured oath, the president bent over and sank the three-ball.

Cavendish disappeared in a rage. It wasn't until the next day, when he was summoned to dinner, that Grant saw his captor again.

"Ah!" Cavendish exclaimed, motioning the president to the opposite end of a long dining table. "Please be seated, Mister Grant."

The president allowed himself to be seated by a Chinese servant. Cavendish was composed, trying hard to display an air of supreme control.

"I've eaten," Cavendish pronounced.

"I'm not hungry."

Cavendish pursed his lips with feigned regret. "Oh, that's a pity," he lamented. "My chef will be extremely disappointed." He swiveled around in his chair. "Lin

Loo, please bring us cigars, then tell the chef that our guest will not be dining at present."

Grant took a cigar, sniffed it cautiously, and decided it was probably a finer brand than he normally smoked.

"I'd like your opinion of this letter, Mister Grant. Besides, since it directly concerns your well being, I think you'll be fascinated by its contents."

"I doubt it very much," the president grated, "but read it anyway."

Cavendish cleared his throat self-importantly and began.

" 'To Mister Hamilton Fish, Secretary of State. Dear Sir: Whereas the government of the United States has failed in its attempts to reconstruct our nation as promised by the Republican party; and whereas it has failed to provide proper protection for American citizens; and whereas it has failed to provide honest leadership and moral courage . . .' "

"Now just a damned minute!" Grant raved, hurling his cigar onto his empty plate and bouncing erect. "I sure as hell don't have to listen to this pack of lies. You are insane, Cavendish!"

The letter shook violently in Cavendish's grasp, but he did not allow his composure to disintegrate as it had the evening before.

"Let's see," he continued. "Yes, here we are, right after 'whereas it has failed to provide honest leadership and moral courage . . . Therefore, let it be known that I, Bartholomew Cavendish, firmly resolve to hold the president of the United States as my prisoner until I am deeded sovereign right of ownership to the lands specified in Exhibit A of this document.' "

He held Exhibit A aloft. "Lieutenant Perlmutter did this. Rather good, isn't it? See how he's used color to delineate my new republic?"

"Your fairytale kingdom! That's all it is, Cavendish!"

"Major Cavendish," came the snapping reply. "And,

163

if you are guilty of one more ill-mannered outburst, I will personally bust your knuckles—one by precious one."

Grant's teeth gnashed together in a quiet rage. He hated this animal! And, for the thousandth time, he cursed the days, years ago, when he'd let Cavendish off with only a dishonorable discharge. He should have been executed by firing squad.

"That's better, Mister Grant. When I'm through reading this historic document, I'll show you my campaign room and the excellent miniature landscape we prepared for yesterday's operation."

He returned to the document. "I was saying that I'd hold you prisoner until I'm deeded sovereign right of ownership to Texas as detailed in this, Exhibit A. 'Furthermore, I demand that this land be granted to me by an irrevocable Act of the Congress of the United States no later than sixty days after this document's receipt. Failure to comply will result—without exception—in the life of Ulysses S. Grant being terminated.' "

He glanced up expectantly.

"It's very good," Grant said, calming his voice.

"You think so?"

"Yes—marvelous, in fact." He relit his cigar and the move steadied him. "But sixty days is too long to give Congress. I'd change that. Hellfire, Cavendish, they'll dicker and debate until it is too late and someone remembers that I'm dead."

"Hmm. Pehaps you're right." Cavendish scratched out *sixty* and wrote *thirty*. "Thank you."

"You're welcome," Grant replied. "It'll be interesting to see what happens."

"Won't it," Cavendish said, happily. Then he leaned far over the table and handed Grant a gold-pointed pen and an ink vial, along with the document. "Sign it, Mister President."

He did. There was really no alternative.

Chapter 16

THE Lone Ranger and Tonto followed Butch Cavendish's trail through the sunset into darkness. At midnight, they finally reached the box canyon that had always eluded Captain Dan Reid and his Texas Rangers. And no wonder. The entrance was almost invisible to the outside world and a perfect trap for anyone who might follow.

"We'd better lead our horses from this point," the Lone Ranger whispered. "We'll hug the rock walls so even moonlight can't expose our position."

Less than ten minutes later, the trail brought them to the fortress itself and they heard the uproarious laughter of a celebration. The Lone Ranger inspected the huge, pointed logs that spanned the narrow canyon.

Tonto pulled his sleeve and pointed upward at the dozing guard who manned the sentry post. He was superbly placed, near the upper righthand side of the gate. He had a complete view of the canyon approach.

The Lone Ranger took a deep breath. So far, they'd been lucky not to have been seen. But now that they'd come this far, how could he and Tonto get inside?

They decided that a distraction was necessary. Tonto started up the right side of the canyon's wall and once he was in position, the Lone Ranger struck a cupped match, then snuffed the flame. Tonto pushed several rocks down into the compound.

The guard snapped to attention.

"Who goes there!"

There was no answer but, since the noise came from within the post, he growled, "Quit fooling around, or I'll come down and put you on report."

They waited another fifteen minutes until the Lone Ranger could hear the guard's snoring. He acted quickly, taking the rope from his saddle and tying it around a boat-shaped rock. He flung the rope up toward the sharp log tips above. The rock encircled a post and fell, banging softly as he eased it down to his reach.

The Lone Ranger held his breath and the muzzle of the great white stallion, knowing that, if the guard chanced to look straight down, they would be discovered instantly.

Tonto dropped more rocks into the compound, distracting the guard, and the Lone Ranger began the next crucial step. He tied one end of the rope to his saddlehorn. He removed the rock from the other end and placed the toe of his boot in the loop.

"All right, big Silver," he whispered, "pull me up!"

Silver nickered softly into his gloved hand, then turned and began to strain against the Lone Ranger's weight. The powerful white stallion moved back from the fortress wall and lifted the Lone Ranger until he was able to swing over the sharp points of the logs.

"I'm a'gettin' damn tired of whoever keeps throwin' those rocks!" came the angry shout.

The Lone Ranger dangled against the inside of the fortress wall. He gripped the sharp posts and desperately waved down at the stallion. For a moment, Silver stared at the man, then slowly approached the wall, the muscles in his haunches tightly bunched as he lowered the weight into the fortress.

Good boy! The Lone Ranger sang to himself as his feet touched the dirt. Then he extracted his boot from the noose and jerked the rope twice as he pressed his face against the logs and whispered, "Take it back, Silver!"

The stallion understood and the rope vanished. The Lone Ranger felt around in the dark until he located a pebble, then tossed it toward the far end of the wall.

"Hey! How many of you are out there foolin' around! I'm going to get the lieutenant to stop this. It's bad enough I have to miss the party without being bedeviled."

Minutes later, the Lone Ranger squeezed the gate bar out of place just long enough for Tonto to slip through. Suddenly, a door burst open somewhere behind them and the compound was flooded with light. The masked man and his friend dropped against the base of the wall and hugged the shadow.

A dancehall girl swayed drunkenly from the bunkhouse. Her dress was rumpled, with a strap torn from one bare shoulder. Through the open doorway, the Lone Ranger and Tonto could see a mass of tightly packed bodies, some erect, some stretched out on the floor in various stages of intoxication. The party, it seemed, was in its last convulsive stages.

"Aw, c'mon, honey. Share another drink with me," a trooper wheedled, as he plowed through the doorway and threw his arm around the girl's waist. She struggled halfheartedly and reached for the bottle of whiskey in his hand. When she'd drunk her fill, the trooper yanked her inside and slammed the door.

In those brief moments, the Lone Ranger had been studying the layout. "Tonto, did you see the size of this compound?"

"Yes, Kemo Sabe. The big house—Cavendish's?"

He'd seen it, too. A huge, two-storied building with an upstairs and downstairs balcony. It looked like a plantation mansion out of the deep South and seemed so out of place in this wild Texas country.

"Probably."

"What do we do now, Kemo Sabe?"

The Lone Ranger peered up at the moon. "It's after midnight. From what I've seen, this party can't last much longer. We'll give everyone time to sleep, then we find them."

"Who?" Tonto asked. "It is important that I know which man you want most—President Grant, or Butch Cavendish. We may have time for only one this night."

The Lone Ranger weighed his answer carefully. To be this close and let Butch Cavendish escape seemed more of a punishment than he could endure. Yet, Tonto was right. If it came down to a choice, his partner deserved an answer; it might mean the difference between living and dying.

"Kemo Sabe. Speak from your heart."

"I can't, Tonto. Since that day at Bryant's Gap, I've lived for this moment when I could repay Cavendish. But now . . . now, I realize that the president's life is more important than my own vendetta."

He gripped his friend's shoulder. "We *must* first think of the president of the United States! If we fail, Cavendish is mad enough to kill Grant tonight. We are the president's only chance."

"This is how it will be?"

"Yes, Tonto."

The Indian nodded, unsheathed his hunting knife. "Come," he said, "the lights are gone and daylight approaches."

They followed the canyon stream that led through the stronghold up toward Cavendish's private domain. During their wait, clouds had pushed against the moon and obscured it from view. Now, a fresh wind brought

170

the first drops of rain as the two men crept forward in the darkness.

Lightning spit a jagged arc in the heavens and, in that one, blinding instant, the Lone Ranger saw a building up ahead and a sign tacked against its walk: DANGER—EXPLOSIVES.

The shed was locked. The Lone Ranger's fingers noted the heft of the big padlock and felt around the stout doorframe. Even the hinges were on the inside! They were out of luck.

Tonto examined the door thoroughly and slid the blade of his hunting knife between the door and its frame. A smile lit his face and, with two quick slashes, he cut the door free and lifted it out of place.

"Leather hinges, Kemo Sabe," he explained as he set the door aside.

"Nice work!" the Lone Ranger said, as he entered the explosives shack.

There was no choice but to light another match, so the Lone Ranger did it from the open doorway. "Look at that!" he exclaimed, pitching the match outside. "There's enough ammunition and dynamite in here to start another Civil War!"

"What now?"

"We use it, Tonto. We rig every inch of this compound before daylight."

In the fading hours before dawn, the pair worked frantically. The guard had grown weary of what he thought was drunken trickery and had fallen asleep. They rigged fuses to everything. The stairs leading up to the bunkhouse. The tackroom. The barn. The blacksmith shop. The corral. And the huge edifice they knew was Butch Cavendish's house. Finally, the Lone Ranger wired ten sticks of dynamite together and placed them in a small wooden box.

Tonto looked confused. "What for?"

"For escape, my friend. When we managed to get the president, we still have to get him through those big gates. With all that's going to be happening, we can't figure the guard will be asleep and, if it's daylight, we'd never get past the gate alive."

He lifted the box and placed it right beside the stream. "Did you saddle three horses and leave them tied in the corral?"

Tonto nodded and moved to connect the fuse that ran from Cavendish's place to the ammunition shed. No matter what happened during the next hour, both of them agreed that the arsenal had to be destroyed.

Tonto placed the fuse beside Cavendish's front steps and signaled that he was ready. They ran together along the side of the massive house until they found a window. Inside, nothing moved except the shadows of the flames from the hearth. They glided silently around the house, peering into the other windows. *Still* no sign of life. Where was the president? And Cavendish? There was only one solution—they had to be upstairs and that meant he and Tonto *must* gain entry.

Together, they began to inspect the bars that protected the windows. It was just like Cavendish to take this final precaution, even in the midst of his own stronghold. The outlaw overlooked nothing!

"Check the door hinges, Tonto."

A moment later the Indian returned. "No luck. They were steel this time."

"Then, we'll . . ."

The words froze in his throat as they heard hoofbeats draw up to the front, then boots thud across the porch.

A key turned in the lock and a voice called, "Anyone up?"

No answer.

"Come on, Rafe. Even the boss has to sleep sometime. Everything is all right."

"Yeah, but . . ."

"But nothin'! We gotta sleep, too. We'll be dog tired in the morning. Let the next watch make inside rounds."

"But I got the keys!"

"Then don't lock the place! Come on, or I'm leaving."

"All right," came the grudging reply. "Hell, it's near daylight anyways."

There was a creaking of leather and the sound of fading hoofbeats.

The Lone Ranger sighed. "Maybe the Great Spirit is with us."

The Indian gazed out at the imposing wall and front gate, at the sentry tower and the dim outline of a guard and his rifle. "The Great Spirit *better* be with us, Kemo Sabe."

They slipped through the front door and tiptoed to the stairway. "Well, here goes," the Lone Ranger whispered. "Let's hope we open the right door the first time."

Upstairs, they crept down the long hallway on the balls of their feet. It was almost totally black, and all the Lone Ranger could do was brush his fingers along the doors, marking which ones were open or closed.

"We are going to have to try a room sooner or later."

"I know." The Lone Ranger placed his palm over a doorknob, took a deep breath, and moved inside.

Moonlight played across the slumbering form of Sheriff Justin A. Wiatt. Another betrayer! He drew a gun and marched up to the bed, then pressed the cold steel of his six-gun between Wiatt's deep-set, traitorous little eyes.

"Time to get up, *Sheriff*."

Wiatt convulsed with fear. Then he realized who held the gun to his face. "Don't kill me!" he begged hoarsely.

"Where's the president!"

"I don't know."

The Lone Ranger cocked the hammer of his revolver just as Tonto reached out and grabbed a fistful of the sheriff's hair and drew his big hunting knife.

"Oh, my God!" Wiatt babbled, nearing hysteria. "Don't do this to me! The president? Is that who you want?"

"Yes."

"Third door down on the left! He's in there. Not here. In there. Don't scalp me, Indian!"

Tonto threw Wiatt's head back on the pillow and grabbed the man's pants, then began to hack them into strips.

"My God!" the Sheriff breathed. "Is he blood lust crazy!"

"Quiet! He's going to gag and tie you. If you make *any* attempt to move or sound a warning, I'll let him in here to lift your scalp. Understand?"

Wiatt started to say, "Yes!" He sure as hell did, but Tonto stuffed a wad of pantsleg into his mouth, then tied him up.

Minutes later, they were standing before the president's bed. "Uh, Mister President. Excuse me, sir, but . . ."

Grant's eyelids fluttered, popped open. His reaction was only slightly less dramatic than Wiatt's. "Holy cow, what now?" he gasped, as he stared in disbelief at the masked man and his Indian companion.

"Don't be alarmed. We're going to help."

"Help? What kinda fool do you take me for? The last thing I need is the help of an outlaw and a renegade Indian."

"I'm no renegade," Tonto said evenly. "I'm a man of honor and you have my promise we are here to help you escape."

"Trust us," the Lone Ranger pleaded.

"I don't trust anybody."

Tonto handed Wiatt's gunbelt to the president of the United States. "If you won't trust us, then you'd better pick up that gun and use it, Mister President, because we'll all die here anyway."

Ulysses S. Grant unholstered the gun and checked

to make sure he wasn't being bamboozled. It was fully loaded and in good working order.

"All right," he said slowly. "I don't understand any of this, but I've got nothing to lose now, so tell me what you want me to do."

The Lone Ranger said, "We want you to get dressed, Mister President. Tonto and I are taking you home."

Grant studied each of them, then he seemed to make up his mind. The deep worry lines in his face vanished and he jammed Wiatt's forty-five back into its holster like a man who was ready to go to war. He hopped out of bed and jumped into his clothes. Now they were ready. Three determined men who had to outwit and maybe outgun all of Cavendish's army to escape with their lives.

They moved quietly down the stairs and out into the beginning of a new day. The sky was clear now, a faint light spreading salmon and gold layers on the eastern mountains. In the corral, horses began to stomp for their morning feed and the scent of firewood rose up from the mess hall over near the south canyon wall.

Time was running out.

"The fuses!" the Lone Ranger whispered urgently. "We'll light them on our way to the horses."

They darted across the open compound, all three lighting the fuses as they ran toward the corral.

"Damn me if this ain't the most fun I've had in years!" Grant grinned, dashing from one cache of dynamite to another.

The Lone Ranger and Tonto looked up from their own fuses and smiled. The president of the United States wasn't such a bad fellow, once he got into the swing of things.

Grant touched off the fuse that would blow up the bunkhouse stairs. "Hope them bastards are right over the top of this when she goes!"

Tonto was the first to reach the stream, and he

found the wooden box with its ten sticks of dynamite all wired and ready. Lighting it quickly, he placed the box into the stream and let it float away, praying that he'd correctly judged the length of fuse so it would explode under the big front gate.

The Lone Ranger watched the president spring from the blacksmith shop. They had to hurry! Any minute, the first charge would go off and then all hell would be popping! If they weren't mounted and . . .

A siren pierced the silence of the compound and filled the canyon with its earsplitting wail. The three men froze in their tracks. The Lone Ranger spotted a guard up on the roof madly cranking the alarm.

"Run for the horses!" he yelled.

Tonto hesitated, "I haven't lit the one to the ammunition shed."

"No time, Tonto. Get to the horses!"

But the president wasn't used to taking orders. With what sounded like a battle cry, Grant ripped Sheriff Wiatt's pistol out of its holster and began shooting wildly up at the siren. Bullets whanged and pinged off the contraption and knocked it flying as its operator dove for cover.

"Soak up lead, you sons of bitches!" Grant roared as the bunkhouse stairs disintegrated in a tremendous explosion.

The Lone Ranger grabbed the president, and all three of them sprinted to the horses and managed to get lined out in a wild ride toward the main gate.

A high-caliber rifle boomed. Grant's horse folded between them, throwing the president headlong into the stream.

"Go on!" he shouted, pushing up onto his elbows. "Get outa here if you can!"

Both the Lone Ranger and Tonto peeled off in opposite directions and circled back toward the fallen rider. The Lone Ranger reached Grant first and flipped him up behind the saddle.

"Wahoo!" President Grant yelled, as they reined in a wide turn.

But the Lone Ranger's smile was gone and a terrible sense of doom filled his heart as he saw the unmistakable face of Butch Cavendish lower itself against the rifle and prepare to fire once more.

The same man. The same death-dealing rifle that never missed. The same fatal ending of Bryant's Gap. A repeating nightmare. Now it was all over.

Chapter 17

"No!" cried the Lone Ranger, firing and reining his mount sharply.

Cavendish's bullet, intended for the masked man's chest, was thrown wide by the Lone Ranger's abrupt change in direction.

Cavendish shouted something and began running. The front of his house exploded and he was thrown to the ground as flames and smoke belched into the sky.

Tonto raced back into the billowing smoke to light the fuse to the ammunition shed.

"Get up there!" the Lone Ranger shouted to the president.

"On top of the water flume?"

"Yes, you'll be safe."

"I don't want to be safe. I can still fight and I want to help you, son. I been in enough battles to understand this is warfare."

"I know, sir, but that's when you were a soldier.

Now you're our president, and you have a nation to lead, so get up on that flume and keep your head *down!*"

Grant finished reloading. "All right. I can potshot 'em up there better anyway!" he shouted triumphantly.

The Lone Ranger, guns ready, kept one eye on the president and the other on the melee of confusion he saw everywhere.

Tonto jumped from his skidding horse, lit the ammunition shed fuse, then remounted on the run as the Cavendish men shouted and fired wildly in the smoke. An instant later, the shed exploded like a hundred tangled cannon, sending men and horses plunging away in panic.

Through the swirling smoke, the Lone Ranger saw Cavendish running wildly toward the bunkhouse, shouting for his men to cover the gate.

They *had* to get out now, or they never would! The Lone Ranger's spirits plunged. Somehow, the fuse on the box of dynamite had gotten wet and spluttered out as it floated downstream. Tonto dove from the saddle and rolled into the water. He relit the fuse and dropped the dynamite box back into the current just as a trooper emerged from the smoke. A lone shot cracked overhead and the man spun to the ground.

"Wahoo!" President Grant yelled from up in the flume. "I got him, and the cavalry is coming! Wahoo!"

The Lone Ranger heard it, then. Heard what only the president, who was high above the din and confusion, could have heard before. A bugle. The most beautiful sound ever heard by a desperate frontiersman.

"Masked man!"

He spun around just as Butch Cavendish raised his weapon, just as the floating box with its ten sticks of dynamite hit the front gate and exploded, hurling everything within fifty yards to the ground and sending a mixture of wood, water, and earth spraying into the sky. The sun went black as the huge cloud of debris lifted, then began to rain down, spearing the earth with splintered timber.

The United States Cavalry came tearing through the ragged opening where the gate had been, with Custer, Hickok, and Buffalo Bill Cody leading the charge.

"Wahoo!" Grant bellowed. "Come on, fellas, there's plenty left for everyone!"

The Lone Ranger saw an isolated figure on a black horse charging out of the hole. He knew Butch Cavendish had escaped. He whistled high and sharp, a sound only the great white stallion would understand. Silver was beside him in an instant.

The Lone Ranger mounted on the run then charged through the splintered wreck of the gate after Butch Cavendish. And the president, from his eagle's perch, heard the cry. "Come on, Silver! Let's go, big fella! Hi Yo, Silver!"

The great white stallion closed the distance between them to fifty yards. He held Silver back as Cavendish began firing. But this time, Cavendish wasn't using the deadly hunting rifle or shooting at an immobile target. One by one, the bullets flew wide until the Lone Ranger saw his quarry hurl the pistol away and bend low in the saddle as he began whipping the black horse. The animal responded with a tremendous burst of speed.

It was a horse race, and now that the Lone Ranger didn't have to worry about one of Cavendish's wild shots hitting the white stallion, he gave the great animal free rein.

Cavendish's horse was a magnificent animal, born and bred to run. Yet, Silver seemed to fly across the land and, with every stride, he closed the distance until they were racing side by side.

The Lone Ranger had dreamt of this moment. He

wasted no time, leaping from his saddle and slamming Cavendish down to the ground.

"You fool!" Cavendish spat, jumping erect as he began to circle with upraised fists. "You should have gunned me in the back just now, when you had the chance."

The Lone Ranger's voice was thick with emotion as he remembered his vow to hunt this man down and have his revenge. "Too easy," he said bitterly.

Cavendish laughed, and the Lone Ranger ducked a whistling overhand and slammed a vicious blow to the jaw that momentarily staggered the major. Cavendish was in fine condition and he twisted around and hammered his fist into the Lone Ranger's stomach. Then they stood toe to toe, taking a punch to give one. Two powerful men, each knowing their lives depended on being victorious.

The Lone Ranger blocked a kick and took a crashing fist over the ear. He felt both legs start to buckle, so he grabbed Cavendish and wrestled him to the dirt, feeling the outlaw's powerful fingertips begin to dig into his throat. He twisted sideways and rolled the heavier man aside and they both staggered erect, gasping for air.

The Lone Ranger doubled him up with a powerhouse uppercut to the belly. It was the hardest punch he had ever thrown and it jerked Cavendish's legs from under him as if he'd been roped and thrown.

The Lone Ranger fell beside him with Captain Dan Reid's gun cocked and pressed against the bridge of Cavendish's arrogant, busted nose. The weapon shook violently in his fist as he began to squeeze the trigger. "You . . . you killed my . . ."

"Pull it, damn you!" Cavendish roared. "I won't crawl for any man!"

He tried. With every fiber in his body, the Lone Ranger willed himself to squeeze the trigger. But he couldn't.

"Do it, man! I'd kill you in an instant."

The Lone Ranger lowered the .45 and his voice was steady now. "I know that, Cavendish. But I *still* believe in the law, and it's up to a judge and jury to decide how a man like you will be punished."

Cavendish sneered. "I've been tried for crimes already, masked man. I'll get off and, when I do, I'll pull my army together again and I'll make it my first order of business to track you down and kill both you and that Indian."

The Lone Ranger struggled inwardly as he tried to keep from changing his mind about taking Cavendish back alive. Only one thing kept him from pulling the trigger, and that was Cavendish's own admission that he'd have spared no mercy had he won just now. Maybe that's what separated the law from the lawless —a killer from a man who lived with respect and decency.

"Get up, Cavendish. I'm taking you back. I want you to see what's left of your army now that the United States Cavalry has taken command. And I want to see your expression when you realize your little empire has fallen!"

And fallen it had. Cavendish gazed stoically at what had been his stronghold—the place where he'd plotted and dreamed of launching his own Republic of New Texas. All gone.

The Lone Ranger saw Perlmutter, Sheriff Justin A. Wiatt, and all the others being shackled. He dismounted and pulled Cavendish down beside the president.

"Well, well, *Major*. Thanks to the masked man and his Indian friend, you are now *my* prisoner."

Cavendish watched as manacles were clamped onto his wrists, then his head lifted and hatred burned through his eyes. "I'll be back, Grant. Nothing can keep me from meeting my destiny of leading Texas."

The Lone Ranger, addressing the president, said,

"He killed ten Texas Rangers. He killed a fine newspaperman in Del Rio. He has killed farmers and ranchers. He would have killed you."

Grant swung to face Cavendish. "Your sins will be paid for in the fires of hell!" he snarled. "Take him away! I want full guard on him during the entire journey back to the federal prison in Washington."

"Yes, Mister President!"

Grant turned to the Lone Ranger. "May I know, sir, to whom I am so indebted?"

"With all due respect to you, Mister President, I do not wish to reveal my name. Besides, my prior identity no longer matters."

"Oh," Grant chuckled, "that's where you're most certainly mistaken, young man! The world needs heroes such as you and Tonto. You shall both receive the Congressional Medal of Honor!"

The Lone Ranger smiled and winked at Tonto, who was standing close beside him. "We are grateful for the honor of serving you, Mister President. But, as for myself, permit me to remain anonymous so that I can continue serving the cause of justice and freedom throughout the west. I hope you understand, sir."

"Not really," Grant said pensively. "But if that's the way you and your friend here want things, I will honor your request. The history books will just have to do without your story."

He looked at Tonto. "I suppose you prefer to remain unrecognized as well."

"Yes, Mister President."

Grant frowned. "Seems like damn little thanks for what you've done for this country."

The Lone Ranger saw the hesitation in Tonto's eyes and he nodded. "Ask, my friend."

"Ask what?" Grant looked from one to the other.

"Only," Tonto ventured, "that you thank us by honoring your treaties with my people. They are sick in heart and body and need your help. All Indians must know that treaties with the Great White Father in Washington will last until the stars fall from our night skies."

Grant was visibly moved. He took a deep breath and looked Tonto straight in the eyes. "I came to this country to give a speech. Already wrote the damned thing. But—well, I'm going to do a lot of rewriting between here and El Paso. And, when I get back to the Capitol, I'll start a full-scale investigation into the whole policy of dealing with the red man. I promise you we *will* begin to honor our treaties, Tonto, knowing and expecting your people will do the same."

Tears glistened in Tonto's eyes. He threw back his shoulders and whispered fervently, "Thank you, Mister President!"

The Lone Ranger shook Grant's hand and pressed a silver bullet into his palm.

"What's this?"

But the Lone Ranger and Tonto were already swinging onto their horses and galloping out of the ruined fort.

Grant turned to Custer. "General, do you have any idea who that masked man really is?"

"Of course," came the automatic reply. "He's . . ." Custer tugged at his beard. "I honestly don't know, Mister President. But, judging from what I've seen, we're going to be hearing a lot more from that pair."

Then, from the hills beyond, they heard the cry that was to become legendary—"Hi Yo, Silver. Away!"

Sixty miles off, in the Texas border town of Del Rio, Amy Striker glanced up suddenly. She'd heard and felt a call that seemed to reach across many miles and touch her in the morning stillness. Amy smiled and finished writing the last few lines of tomorrow's front-page editorial:

His face was hidden by a mask, a man no one knew. He rode the plains with his Indian companion, fighting for law and order in those early days of the great West. Now, all the Texas Rangers were dead—only one survived—the one who became known as the Lone Ranger.

THE MYSTERY
BEYOND THE TRINITY

Tripura Rahasya

James Bender Swartz

Shining World Press

Shining World Press is dedicated
to the dissemination of spiritual wisdom.

Shining World Press is located at:
1151 Shattuck Avenue
Berkeley, California, 94707
(510) 559-8055

119 Seshadri Madam
Ramana Nagar
Tiruvannamalai 606603
Tamil Nadu
South India

to contact the author by e-mail:
swartzjb@aol.com
tmalai@md3.vsnl.net.in

ISBN 0-9674444-1-1

This text is dedicated to
Ramana Marharshi,
the sage of Arunachala

INTRODUCTION

Twenty years ago on one of my frequent trips to India I visited the ashram of the sage Ramana Maharshi. The ashram is situated at the foot of a famous Indian holy mountain, Arunachala, in Tamil Nadu a little over one hundred miles south of Madras, now Chennai, in an arid primitive landscape where summer temperatures regularly surpass one hundred degrees. In those days Ramana, who died in the Fifties and had been internationally famous during his lifetime, was largely forgotten (if the number of visitors to the ashram was any indication), although today it is a thriving pilgrimage center. The ashram was a small, quiet, unpretentious affair and a modest, cobwebbed, none-too-clean ten rupee room could be had for the asking at the office. In the bookstore I found a dusty copy of Tripura Rahasya, The Mystery Beyond the Trinity, a Sanskrit text of indeterminate origin, translated into English. The translator said that it had been one of Ramana's favorites so I dutifully purchased it for a few rupees...the equivalent of about a dollar...if memory serves.

Because of an inordinate and inexplicable love of Vedic culture and a patient nature, I struggled through the text and was suitably impressed by the Yogic and Vedantic ideas and the charming

Pauranic style. The Pauranas,[1] a brilliant invention of the *rishis*, India's mystic seer-poets, managed to revive the Vedas, the foundation of Indian spiritual culture, just as they were about to be forgotten.

The Pauranas are called Dharma Shastras, scriptures on Dharma, the Eternal Way. The Pauranas are "the Vedas in action" my guru said. "Vedas in action" means that the cryptic Vedic mantras, which require considerable dedication and brain power to decipher even when unfolded by a sage, were turned into action-packed stories, delightful cartoons appealing to a wide range of minds. The Pauranas were the *rishi's*[2] 'stealth' technology because Upanishadic ideas about the nature of Reality were cleverly hidden behind the exciting, baroque and romantic facade of Pauranic myth. The confounding abundance of Gods that shock and bewilder India's modern visitor are Pauranic deities.

I decided to rework Tripura Rahasya for several reasons. First, to make it more readable in English. The translation from Sanskrit was credible

---

1. *Purana* means ancient and refers to the spiritual literature that followed the Vedic Age (from about 200 BC to the present).
2. A sage or seer. Someone who has "seen" the Truth. Pronounced 'ree she.'

but inevitably suffered from lack of precision - as second-language works often do. Precision is important because Vedantic ideas are often subtle and technical. Although I don't know Sanskrit grammar I know Vedanta reasonably well. Furthermore, my spiritual teacher was a Sanskrit scholar who conducted Vedanta classes in English, so I learned most of the important Vedantic Sanskrit by heart in the two years I sat at his feet. Vedanta is best in Sanskrit but in the last analysis the ideas, and the skill with which they are communicated, not the language in which they're rendered, reveal the mystery beyond the trinity. Tripura Rahasya showcases some very important ideas.

I could have chosen a more famous text but the fact that the guru is a woman, at least in the section I reworked, appealed to me. Vedic culture, not without justification, has recently been accused of sexism. Like the author of Tripura Rahasya, who was undoubtedly male but who chose to let the Vedanta flow from the mouth of a woman, I wanted to make the statement that women are equally capable of realizing the highest truths.

Increasingly, the great spiritual figures of the age are women and, considering the numerous scandals perpetrated of late by men, probably more

iii

worthy of our respect. Although only a 'mere woman' according to her disciple husband, Tripura Rahasya's *rishi* has her act together.

I also decided to 'improve' the text, an idea bound to raise eyebrows in orthodox quarters. Obviously I don't see scripture as set in stone, not for want of devotion to spiritual culture, but because time is no respecter of Truth. Much of what passes for Spirit, our own Bible, for example, is often times a peculiar amalgam of truth, fantasy, projected unconscious content, and blatant opinion. Whether scripture comes in pure and is slowly adulterated or whether it's adulterated from the beginning one cannot say. Nonetheless, I prefer to think of spiritual literature, with notable exceptions, as works in progress, transcendent ideas passing through the human mind, and hence in need of objective editing. It is up to those who respect Truth to purify sacred texts. Failure to do so will undoubtedly result in an even more disturbed world than the one we have now. I think a case could be made that many of history's most blatant religious excesses have been justified on the basis of a literal interpretation of unpurified scripture.

Fortunately the translation that came to me in Ramana's bookstore was remarkably clean. Yet it needed a little work. So I fleshed out some of the ideas, removed linguistic extravagances, archaic metaphors, and redundant examples, which are characteristics of Pauranic literature, and clarified concepts that were perhaps difficult for the translator. When common sense and logic permitted, I also added a few auxiliary teachings which are well within the grand traditions of Vedanta and Yoga. May God have mercy on my soul.

Perhaps I must also plead guilty to the great sin of our age - pandering to the need for entertainment; I spiced and spruced up the relationship between the guru and disciple a bit. In my defense, I got a lot of help from the author who chose the throes of sexual passion as the event that inspired the teachings. One might expect to find such a scenario in touchy-feely New Age literature, but hardly in Vedanta, a discipline so lofty it never deigns to delve into the murky recesses of biology. Of course life is never about what life is about on the surface, and true to form Tripura Rahasya merely uses this dramatic example to lead us into a discussion of the quest for liberation through Self knowledge.

I have not actually reworked the entire text although, in addition to another rather farfetched story meant to illustrate the relatively of time and the power of the mind to create reality, it contains marginally important creation theories, the relationship between the dream and waking state, and other interesting and sometimes advanced spiritual ideas. The part I chose, however, deals with issues that any serious seeker will eventually need to confront. It also insists that enlightenment requires disinterested and professional help and suggests that love problems can be solved in an internal way, with a minimum of egoistic squabbling and marriage counselors. Considering the haphazard character of modern questing and the sorry state of gender relations today, I thought these to be timely messages.

I have included footnotes explaining technical Vedantic words and ideas that may provide additional information to those who wish to delve more deeply into the mystery beyond the trinity.

THE MYSTERY
BEYOND THE TRINITY

Salutations to the blissful non-dual Om,[1] the transcendental Consciousness in which the wonderful universe is mirrored.[2]

Salutations to the undifferentiated and limitless Om that is worshipped as the supreme Goddess in whose luminous crystal-pure body all phenomena live and move and have their being.

Salutations to the Self, the mystery beyond the waking, dream and deep sleep states.[3]

---

1. A sound symbol of undifferentiated pure Consciousness.
2. Consciousness, the cause of all phenomena, is not separate from the phenomena just as a reflection in a mirror is not separate from the mirror.
3. The 'trinity' referred to in the title.

I will now tell you, Oh seeker, the gospel of the illustrious Goddess which teaches the way to transcendence.

The Goddess is called Tripura, mistress of the three cities[4] and 'mother of the universe.'[5]

Goddess worship purifies the mind and creates zeal for inquiry into Truth. Those fit for this discourse on wisdom will be freed from misery.

Though I have realized it, it is not mine.

It is the essence of the Vedas[6] and helps sincere seekers re-discover the essential Self just as a sense of smell allows one to appreciate the fragrance of flowers.

Miserable are those unable to grasp it.

---

4. The three (*tri*) 'cities' (*puri*) symbolize the waking, dream and deep sleep states of Consciousness. The Goddess, a symbol of the undifferentiated Om, 'rules' these cities in the sense that our waking, dream and deep sleep states depend on the association of undifferentiated Consciousness with the gross, subtle and causal bodies. The teaching on Om, the three bodies and three states is given in the Mandukya Upanishad.

5. Consciousness is often symbolized as a mother because love binds it to the universe just as a mother is bound to her children in love. Secondly, Consciousness is the cause of the universe as parents are the cause of children.

6. In this context Vedas means the Upanishads, the appended portions of the Vedas. The Upanishads are the source of Vedanta, an ancient means of knowledge that reveals the limitless Self.

No teaching will impress the mind as much as this. Born of his own experience and validated by scripture, it was first given by the illumined master Dattatreya to his disciple, the pure-minded Parasurama, whose devotional rapture as he listened reached such intensity that his hair stood on end and his skin shivered with joy."

His voice breaking, the disciple said, "Blessed am I that the Supreme Being has incarnated as my gracious Guru who for unknown reasons has just revealed the mystery of the Goddess Tripura.[7] Kindly tell me, Master, how should I worship Her?"

Much to Parasurama's delight Dattatreya carefully explained the sacred meditations and rituals appropriate to Goddess worship.

When the instructions were completed, the disciple bowed, circumambulated the Guru, took the dust of his lotus feet,[8] and set off for a holy

---

7. The disciple has just received *darshan*, an experience of the Self in the form of the Goddess, through his guru. *Darshan* literally means 'sight' or 'vision.'

8. '*Guru*' means 'one who removes darkness' i.e. the 'light' of Self knowledge. 'Feet' symbolize understanding, the knowledge of the Self. Touching the feet represents surrender to the idea of enlightenment. The lotus is a common symbol of enlightenment.

mountain where he built a small hut and enthusiastically worshipped the Goddess for twelve years.

As the years passed Parasurama's devotional exuberance waned and he became increasingly contemplative. He often found himself thinking, "Where does this wonderful world come from? Why does it exist? It seems permanent but is constantly changing. Is it real? Does it ever end?

And what about me? I seem to have been many different people playing many roles, but part of me seems to be exactly the same as always. Who am I?

I have done so many things with the idea that I would become happier yet I am no happier now than ever. If hard work and life experience does not bring lasting happiness, what does?

And who is this Goddess I have been worshipping so long? Sometimes I think she is just a projection of my mind, not a real Being."

Unable to resolve his doubts, Parasurama left his little hut, descended the mountain and set off to find his guru. After

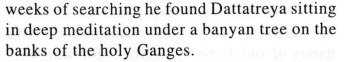

weeks of searching he found Dattatreya sitting in deep meditation under a banyan tree on the banks of the holy Ganges.

He approached the guru's radiant form, touched the revered lotus feet and stepped back, his hands joined prayerfully. The Guru came out of his meditation, smiled and said, " Ah, ha! You are back after all this time. How are you?"

"I am happy to be back," Parasurama answered enthusiastically. "Just the sight of you refreshes me. My worship of the Goddess was very rewarding, but over the years I have started to think about things in a different way. May I ask some questions?" [9]

"Why not?" Dattatreya replied. "If I know the answers I will be happy to tell you."

Dattatreya motioned for him to sit and encouraged him to open his heart.

---

9. Parasurama is mature and free of psychological problems. He is mildly disillusioned with spiritual practice, but on balance he is a positive, centered person whose questions are motivated by curiosity and deep thought. In the Vedic spiritual world he would be condidered an *adikhari*, someone qualified for Self-Realization.

"When I was young," Parasurama began, "our *brahmin* caste suffered gross injustices at the hands of our *kshetriya* rulers. Burning with indignation, I vowed to right these wrongs and set out to exterminate every *kshetriya* in the country.[10] For many years I killed every one I came across, including women and children. The ancestors were eventually pleased with my devotion but ordered me to desist. Finally, my wrath was appeased.

Life returned to normal. Then one day I heard of a famous *kshetriya* living in nearby Ayodhya who was said to be an incarnation of *Dharma*, one Rama by name. I thought my anger was gone but the very mention of his name sent me into a blind fury and I challenged him to battle.[11]

10. In ancient Vedic culture the *brahmins* occupied the highest niche in the caste system because of their learning and spiritual wisdom. The *kshetriya* (political and military) class was required by caste *dharma* to protect and support the *brahmins*. Failure to do so was considered *adharmic*, a serious breach of social obligation.

11. On the esoteric level Rama symbolizes the Self although the average Indian considers him a god or an historical figure. At this stage of life the very idea of the Self made Parasurama angry. One might say he was an atheist.

Though I was considered the most powerful warrior in the land Rama was much more skillful and easily defeated me. Since it was well-known I had slaughtered so many *kshetriya*s, I was certain he would kill me, but he was completely free of pride and ironically chose to let me go because I was a *brahmin*[12].

I had assumed that all *kshetriya*s were beasts because of the way my family had been treated, but Rama was different. He fought with great courage and, surprisingly, without a trace of anger. When he let me go I was ashamed and humiliated. But I also felt a strange admiration and wondered if what they said about him being an incarnation was true.

Although I could not be sure, I was convinced that I would never be caught in the grip of anger again. Yet, I was confused and depressed because my all-consuming passion, revenge, was gone. On the way home I happened upon the great *avadhut*,[13] Samvarta,

---

12. As an incarnation of *Dharma,* Rama would necessarily show mercy to a defeated enemy.

13. *Avaduts* are Self realized souls completely free of body consciousness who wander about naked. They have no fixed abode, don't touch money, nor do they beg for food. They are the highest stage of *sannyasis* (renunciates). *Sannyas* is the forth or final stage of life in the Vedic system.

sitting in meditation under a great banyan tree in the forest. As I am sure you know, though he is only a human being, his *tapas*[14] was so powerful he rendered Indra, the King of the Gods, impotent for trying to disrupt a sacrifice.[15]

His body was smeared with ash and his spirit glowed like a red hot coal. Just being near him filled me with a strange exhilaration. The waves of peace emitting from him washed away the disturbing feelings from my defeat at Rama's hands.

I asked about his state and he said he had merged with the Absolute. When I told him about my Goddess worship, he said that the fruits of ritual worship were limited and that I would have to keep doing my *upasanas*[16] forever to keep my mind quiet. His presence was so overwhelming I felt like a

---

14. The heat or power generated from meditation.
15. The inner meaning is that meditation renders the mind impotent. Indra is a Vedic symbol of the mind. Vedic science also claims that the human level is superior to the level of the Gods because enlightenment is only possible in human form. The state of 'the Gods' is a state of pure pleasure devoid of discrimination. One remains in it until one's good karma runs out. Then the 'God' returns to the human level where it is possible to seek the truth.
16. Religious rituals and detailed meditations found in the Vedas and Pauranas. Spiritual practice does not produce lasting happiness.

beggar before a king and was too impressed to question him properly. It probably would not have made any difference because I think he was too lost in his state to be a good teacher. For weeks his words confused my mind.

I lost interest in devotional practice when I realized it was not going to give answers to the questions troubling me. And I saw that ritualism never ends. Devotion, *bhakti*,[17] seems as imperfect as *karma*[18] as a path to happiness. Finally, I began to meditate on death which led to the conclusion that everything we do here is ultimately pointless.

My meeting with Samvarta made me realize how far a human being can go spiritually. Everything he does is natural and spontaneous. They say he wanders fearlessly through the jungles in the dead of night. He is like a majestic elephant playing in a lake of melted snow while the surrounding forest

17. Devotional practice. Although the path of *karma* does not, *bhakti*, one-pointed love of God, can lead to liberation, lasting happiness. Tripura Rahashya is a Vedantic text, intended for the intellectually inclined. Because of his *bhakti* for the Goddess, Parasurama's intellect has become subtle and inquiring and he now needs a path that can removed his doubts. When one loves someone or something, one desires to know more about it.
18. The belief that lasting fulfillment can come through activity.

burns. How did he gain that state? Please explain these things and rescue me from the jaws of the monster of *karma*."

***

Dattatreya listened with interest and replied, "What you have said shows that you are fit for wisdom. Because of virtuous actions and an open mind, the Goddess, who dwells in the hearts of all and knows their most pressing needs, has sent you to me for help in scaling the sacred mountain of Self realization.

Listen carefully.[19]

Action itself is never a problem. How can we live without action? But the compulsion to act, the fear that unless one engages in both obligatory and discretionary actions one will not be happy, is a thief in the night making off with your most valuable possession...peace of mind. Working for the wrong

---

19. Vedanta is known as a *shabda pramana*, a means of knowledge that uses sound (*shab*) or words to effect enlightenment. Since Parasurama is an *adhikari*, he should easily realize the Self simply by listening attentively to the words of his guru.

reasons with the wrong attitude, humans have lost the power to distinguish what is ultimately good from what is expedient. Therefore, their minds are incapable of inquiry into Truth...like the tired and hungry man who mistook poisonous wild mushrooms for edible ones. The poison caused blindness and he lost his way, eventually stumbling into a river where he was eaten by a crocodile. To be eaten by the crocodile of desire and obligation is the fate of those who lose their discrimination searching for happiness in objects and activities.

Fortunately you have transcended this distracted state and are now capable of making an investigation into your own nature. **Inquiry is the cause of liberation, a seed that will flourish into a gigantic tree of lasting happiness.** Inquiry leads to discrimination and discrimination, separating the real from the apparent,[20] to liberation.

Certainly you know the story from the Ramayana. Because of his attachment to his wife's desires, Rama, the Self, temporarily loses discrimination and fails to heed the wise advice of

---

20. What is seen or known is apparent and the Knower or Seer is Reality. Rediscovery of oneself as the Self, the Seer, is liberation.

his brother. Because of this lapse, Ravana, the ten-headed[21] ego monster, steals Sita by subterfuge. Sita means "peace" and stands for a pure mind, one wedded to the Self. To regain his peace of mind Rama, with the help of *bhakti*, (Hanuman), wars with and ultimately kills the ravenous ego.[22] Had he used discrimination in the first place much suffering would have been avoided.

Inquiry,[23] life's most valuable possession, is the royal road to Self realization. I was concerned when you left twelve years ago after your vision of the Goddess because you were acting only on your devotional feelings. I took care to teach you how to worship properly so that you would develop an

---

21. The ten heads represent the five active and five perceptive senses.

22. This story, perhaps the most famous and poetic Paurana, is known to nearly every Indian. In the old days it was repeated endlessly by village storytellers. A forty part television series of the Ramayana was the most popular television show ever and brought the whole country to a standstill during screenings.

The Indian mind's lack of a linear chronological sense is probably responsible for the mention of Rama as a mythological figure and his subsequent appearance in the life of Parasurama.

23. *Vichara* in Sanskrit. It also means investigation, discernment, and discrimination.

inquiring mind. You have become self-aware because of your meditations on the Goddess. For those who worship Her become rich in love and brilliant of mind.

"But surely, the Goddess blesses many in this way. Are there other factors necessary for liberation?" Parasurama replied.

"Very good!" Dattatreya said, impressed by the question. Association with the wise leads to Self inquiry. Inquiry is not simply asking questions like 'Who am I,' 'What is the cause of the universe?,' 'Why am I suffering?' and waiting or praying for an answer. It is a process of discrimination, comparing the ego with the Self, accepting the knowledge that you are whole and complete and allowing it to percolate into every aspect of your being until the mind is transformed and your feelings and actions harmonize with the Truth."

"What do you mean by 'the knowledge that I am whole and complete?' said Parasurama.

"People under the spell of ignorance think of themselves as limited, inadequate, incomplete beings. Because this is merely an ill-considered opinion and not a fact, they suffer. The more they cling to this notion the more disturbed they become, until everything they do reinforces this belief. A change of habits, devotional practice, meditation, or intellectually asking 'Who am I?' will not remove this fundamental error.

But changing the platform from which you view yourself by seeing yourself as adequate, whole and complete will cause your thought and feeling life to gradually shift and eventually synchronize with your real nature. All that separates you from your Self is the erroneous notion that you are incomplete and inadequate. Discrimination, because it blows away the cloud of unknowing veiling the Self, allows you to stand free of your fears and desires. When your mind is free it can easily realize the Self.

Association with a realized soul lets you see how his or her Self knowledge translates into an efficient and happy life. Slowly the vision transfers to you."

"I thought the whole point of spiritual practice, meditation especially, was to stop thinking altogether. Do not our ancient *yoga* texts say

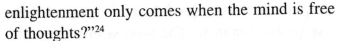

enlightenment only comes when the mind is free of thoughts?"[24]

"There is truth to that view," Dattatreya replied, "because one cannot conduct a proper inquiry into oneself until the mind is psychologically sound, relatively free of disturbing thoughts and feelings. But thought is natural to human beings, a function in consciousness...like breathing. And the Self is beyond the mind, unaffected by thought or the absence of thought. The Self does seem to automatically appear when the mind is still, but

---

24. Some argue that because the Self is already realized, only the unenlightened mind/ego entity can get enlightened. Others say that since only the Self exists there is no ego to get enlightened. These apparently opposing views suggest that ignorance both exists and does not exist. The problem is resolved by determining which point of view is operating. From the Self's point of view ignorance and ego do not exist, except as illusion, or not at all if the mind is completely destroyed. From the ego's point of view, ignorance exists (because it sees itself as inadequate, incomplete, and limited). If you argue that limitation is natural to the ego how do you explain ego's continual desire to rid itself of it? Furthermore, when the ego experiences oneness with the Self it clings to the experience tooth and nail, suggesting that oneness is its nature. An ego that has never 'experienced the Self' does not know it is ignorant of the Self. The teachings of Vedanta are meant to help egos who know they are ignorant remove their ignorance.

The Mystery Beyond the Trinity

keeping the mind free of thoughts is not possible, except momentarily. The process of inquiry uses the mind's power to 'lift it out of itself' or 'experience the Self.' And since it is the mind that gets enlightened, it must remain awake and alert for the knowledge of the Self to dawn in it. A mind without thought is not a mind. When the experience of emptiness, which is just another dualistic experience, ends, ignorance reasserts itself and all one's limitations return."

"I think I understand, said Parasurama, "but is not a new way of thinking just another limiting factor?"

"Yes, but this kind of thinking is different. When the stomach is upset with too much acid, a base is taken. When the base neutralizes the acid, neither remains. The thought that I am whole and complete neutralizes the thought that I am incomplete and inadequate, leaving the mind free of confining thoughts. In a mind free of limiting concepts the ever-free Self is realized."

Thinking is not a problem. We need the mind to take care of many things in life. The only unhealthy thought is, 'I am a limited being'"

"But surely this is not a conscious thought?"

"Correct!" said Dattatreya, impressed by his disciple's insight. "It is unconscious, hidden behind the screen of daily thinking. The purpose of inquiry is to expose this thought (which we take for the truth) and replace it with the truth...'I am limitless being. I am effortless awareness. I am the Self.' In fact, there is nothing to replace. When you transcend the mind, the Self, the mind's substrate, is realized.

But let me return to the point about association with the wise. If you analyze your experience you will see that you had contact with Rama, Samvarta, and me. Before you met us you were an atheistic, angry, violent young man, heading for destruction. Rama's compassion turned you around and made you think about what you were doing. Samvarta gave you a deep experience of the Self which made you question the way you were living.

Let me tell a story that shows the importance of associating with *mahatmas*.[25]

_____

25. 'Great souls' or Self realized beings.

One day, a learned and cultured prince became separated from his hunting party in a wild forest and stumbled upon a clearing. To his amazement he saw a beautiful, radiant, peaceful young woman sitting in front of a small grass hut.

When he approached and asked who she was she welcomed him with great courtesy saying, "Hospitality is the sacred duty of the pious."

He realized that in spite of her humble surroundings and common dress she was a cultured person.

She offered refreshment and told her story. "My name is Hemalekha and I am the foster child of Nyaghrapada, a sage of unparalleled wisdom," she said.

"I am the actual daughter of a beautiful celestial damsel, Vidyadhari[26] who came to a nearby river to bathe one day. It so happened that a nobleman who was passing saw her and immediately fell in love. She returned his love and became pregnant but

---

26. 'The one who loves knowledge.'

he ran off and left her alone - as men are likely to do. She was afraid of slander and caused an abortion, but I was born alive and placed on the river bank."

"Nyaghrapada came to the river for evening prayers and took me home because of his love for sentient beings. Our scriptures say that the one who offers righteous protection is the father. I am therefore his daughter and devoted to him."

"But are not you afraid to live alone in the forest," Hemachuda asked.

"Not at all," she replied. "The sage is very powerful. Not even gods or demons, much less mere mortals, can enter this hermitage if they harbor selfish motives. Wait here. The sage is gathering flowers for his worship. When he returns, humbly ask for shelter and I am sure he will let you stay the night."

At some point during Himalekha's story the prince fell hopelessly in love and his mind became extremely agitated. Fearing that his feelings might cause her offense he tried to conceal them but she picked up on them and said, "I understand your feelings, prince. Tell my father everything and see what happens."

Realizing she shared his feelings to some extent, the prince relaxed. When the sage arrived, carrying a basket of flowers for his worship, the prince rose, prostrated, introduced himself and took his seat at the sage's direction. Assessing the situation with his occult powers, Nyagrhapada said, "I see that you are in love with my daughter. You have my permission to marry her. Treat her well for she is much more than you, in your distracted state, think."

Though he did not know what the sage meant, the prince was overjoyed and returned to the palace with Hemakekha the next morning. The king and queen were also pleased and ordered a week's festivities culminating in a grand wedding.

On the wedding night the couple retired to the nuptial chamber to consummate the marriage, the prince wild with excitement. As he became more and more aroused he realized his wife's mood did not match his own. In fact, she seemed quite unresponsive. So he stopped his lovemaking and said, "What is the matter, dear? Is not this greatest of pleasures to your taste? You seem quite indifferent. How can I be happy if you are uninterested in sex? You seem almost unconscious and, incredibly, you even asked, "My Lord, are you finished?" I doubt that you even heard the wonderful things I said to you. To be honest, I am terribly disappointed. This has been one of the most unpleasant experiences of my life. What is the matter?"

Hemalekha looked at him with amusement, a slight smile on her face, but said nothing.

Clearly distraught, the prince said, "Please speak! Why are you like this? You are more dear to me than my own life. Please relieve my mind!"

Seeing her infatuated husband's distress, Hemalekha said, "It is not that I do not love you, but every minute I am trying to find a joy that will not eventually become a source of frustration. Perhaps this is why I seem distracted. I am sure there is such a joy but I am not exactly sure what it is. It can not be sex, can it, since one always seems to need more of it? Perhaps you know what it is and will help me find it. "

Hemachuda laughed derisively and said, "Are you serious? You are a typical woman, slightly short of brains. Even animals know what is good and bad. Whatever feels good is good and what feels bad is bad!"

"It is true women are foolish, lacking in common sense," Hemalekha replied with a touch of sarcasm. "How kind of you to correct my thinking so I can enjoy this 'greatest of pleasures' with the same heedless passion that seems to motivate you. This will make for a very happy marriage, I am sure."

Hemachuda was shocked and confused by his wife's attitude. No one had ever spoken to him in this manner and he was unable to reply.

Hemalekha continued, "If it is true that getting what you want is happiness and avoiding what you do not want is unhappiness, then why does an object that formerly gave happiness often bring unhappiness? You were quite happy with me as a woman until you discovered that I do not share the same interest in sex that you do. Now you are quite unhappy with me, ridiculing as foolish and stupid the very woman that only a few hours ago you vowed to honor and protect for as long as you live."

"Or take a less personal example. In the winter fire gives pleasure, in the summer discomfort. This leads to the conclusion that pleasure and pain are controlled by circumstances, not personal will. Everything that can be possessed

Tripura Rahasya

and enjoyed changes. If it does not change, then you change. You become dissatisfied and your relationship with it changes."

"If what feels good is happiness, then why is not your father happy? He can instantly have any pleasure known to man. Yet, he is full of desires, as if he has nothing at all. Every minute he is trying to get something he thinks he lacks."

Hemachuda, amazed at the depth of his wife's understanding, saw his anger change to admiration.

She continued, "I think that happiness associated with objects and activities, the kind that can change to unhappiness or indifference, is not real happiness. Anyone who thinks that satisfying desires will lead to happiness is mistaken. In fact desire is a sign of unhappiness."

"Take sex, for example. Why do you want sex? Because you are tortured by lust. Sex is not really what you want. After all, what is it but two pieces of meat rubbing together? What you want is the freedom from the misery of lust. But sex does not diminish the pain of lust - except temporarily. Quite the contrary, the more sex one has, the more lust increases."

"Or beauty. Every day people fall in love with something or someone they find attractive because they think it will bring happiness. Yet beauty is not in any object. If it were, the same object would make everyone who possessed and enjoyed it happy. Let me tell you a story to illustrate my point".

"A handsome king was very devoted to his equally beautiful wife. But the wife loved a servant in the royal household. She had the servant get the king very drunk every evening and call in a prostitute who showed the king a good time while the queen carried on with the servant. The king thought he was the happiest of men to be married to such a wonderful woman."

"One night, however, the servant, eager to get to the queen, neglected to stay until the king was sufficiently drunk. He enjoyed himself for a while but the alcohol wore off before he passed out and he discovered the ruse."

"When he threatened the woman she confessed. He ran to the queen's chambers and found her locked in the embrace of the loathsome servant. Realizing the vanity of his ways the king abandoned his duties and went off in search of God."

"At least some good came of it," Hemachuda said.

"Perhaps," said Hemalekha, "but I think it interesting that the king was happy as long as he thought the prostitute was his wife. But when he discovered otherwise his happiness deserted him. **This shows that what really made him happy was acting out the mental concept associated with his desire** and not the queen nor the love making itself."

"I do not understand," her husband replied. "Please explain."

"Based on the memory of previous pleasant experiences, the mind creates a fantasy which it would like to enjoy," Hemakekha began. "The more it thinks about its fantasy, the more it becomes enslaved to it. When the pain of enslavement is too great to bear, the fantasy has to become reality. So it is directed to a real person. The fantasy exerts a magnetic attraction on the object. Who can resist the appearance of so much need? If the projection works and the fantasized object succumbs, the relationship will be unsuccessful because people need to be taken for what they are, not as objects of other's desires. Each of us needs to know that we are valuable apart from the projections of others."

If you want to make love with me and you want me to respond, then **you need to find out who I am.** What pleasure is there for me if I know that you are only making love with the idea that women are meant to satisfy men's lust? Real love is when you love the beloved for the beloved's sake, not simply for what she can do for you. If you loved me for my sake you would take time to find out who I am."

Hemachuda, who had been following the argument carefully, suddenly felt ashamed.

Hemalekha continued, "Even if this idea is incorrect, consider carefully what you actually think is the source of sexual pleasure."

"Take a look at this," she said, pointing to her body. "Just what part do you love? The hair? Dead protein. The bones? Only calcium. And what about the lower half, the part that seems of special interest to men? Should we talk about the blood, the mucus, the feces and urine, not to mention the host of tiny organisms that live and breed and die inside?"

A look of disgust and comprehension crossed Hemachuda's face and Hemalekha knew she had made her point.

Hemachuda was absolutely amazed at Hemalekha's strange discourse. When he fell in love he had no idea she was so self-contained and such a deep thinker. His admiration increased and he thought carefully about everything she said. Over time his interest in worldly pleasures waned - yet desire remained and he found himself unable to either enjoy himself or to let go of the cravings completely, his mind swaying to and fro like a swing. The constant struggle sapped his energy and he became sad and depressed.

"You seem distracted these days," his wife said. "What is the matter?"

"As if you do not know," he said dejectedly. "Your words brought on this state. Nonetheless I am not angry with you. I am like a condemned man unable to enjoy his last dinner. Since you got me into this sorry state, maybe you can help me out of it. I want my happiness back."

"Yes, you are right. My well-chosen words brought this favorable reaction."

"Favorable reaction?" Hemachuda replied sarcastically. "You must be joking. This is not a pleasant state of mind."

"I know that, but had you simply ignored what I had to say and continued your blind pursuit you would have been unfit for the Gospel."

"The Gospel? What Gospel?"

"The teachings of the Goddess Tripura, the science of Self-Knowledge, the only sure way to lasting happiness."

"This is preposterous. Will you stop pulling my leg? Are you now claiming to possess that supreme happiness that is spoken of in our ancient scriptures?"

"Perhaps it does seem preposterous that a mere woman should be enlightened, but you might recall that I am the daughter of a celestial and that I was raised by the omniscient sage, Nyagrhapada."

"But the morning after our wedding night you said that you were still seeking lasting happiness. Now you say you have it? What am I to believe?"

"I am sorry I deceived you," Hemalekha said. "But I thought it would have been a little too much for you to accept at first. That is why I started the

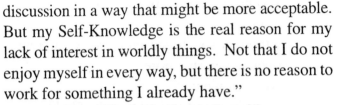

discussion in a way that might be more acceptable. But my Self-Knowledge is the real reason for my lack of interest in worldly things. Not that I do not enjoy myself in every way, but there is no reason to work for something I already have."

"Something you already have?"

"People pursue pleasure for the happiness it brings, not for the pleasure itself. When you are already happy, why chase pleasure?"

"What you say is logical, but could it really be true? Do you really feel happy all the time?"

"It is not exactly happy as opposed to unhappy, but a sense of being complete and whole - not needing anything. I experience pleasure and pain like you, but I do not seek pleasure or try to avoid pain. I take what comes with a grain of salt because I know that ultimately nothing can change me...for better or for worse. I am satisfied with what I am."

"Again, I am sorry I deceived you but you would not have believed me in that emotionally charged moment. I know you have no way of knowing whether or not what I say is true, and I may have made things worse by deceiving you, but I think you realized that what I said about sex and love was true."

"It is hard to admit, but yes, you are right. It did make sense."

"I thought so. It caused a change and now you are open to hearing more."

"More of what?"

"The Gospel of my mother the Goddess Sri Tripura."

"I think I have heard enough already. Look at the state your wisdom has put me in."

"Yes, that is true, but the Gospel also shows the way out."

"What is the way out? I will do anything to get out of this state."

"First you need to understand why you are as you are, why you have forgotten your original nature. Let me tell you my true story.

"My Mother,[27] a great queen, gave me to one of her ladies in waiting, a very pure woman[28] whom I loved more than life itself. I could not remain without her even for even a few minutes. This woman, however, loved Madame Ignorance,[29] a

---

27. The Self, pure limitless Consciousness.
28. The indvidual Self or pure ego.
29. *Maya*, Self forgetfulness or ignorance.

wicked strumpet who was forever creating new and exciting things. Because of my attachment to the lady in waiting, who was like a sister to me, I also associated with her friend behind my Mother's back."

"That wicked woman secretly introduced her son, an ignorant drunk, one Mr. Fool,[30] to my friend, who openly carried on the most unseemly affair with him. Needless to say, I was shocked and disgusted, but I would not leave her because I was very attached to her. Before long they had a child who was named Master Inconstant.[31] This child inherited his father's stupidity and his grandmother's creative wickedness. Under their tutelage he grew up to be a restless fellow skilled in their ways. He could negotiate the most difficult places with perfect ease and surmount obstacles in a trice."

"Because of her association with Madame Ignorance, Mr. Fool, and Master Inconstant, my friend gradually lost interest in me but I was young and needy so I stayed around anyway. Mr. Fool, a lusty fellow who was continually having intercourse

---

30. The ego. The part that is intoxicated with life.
31. The intellect.

with his wife, thought I was like her and repeatedly tried to rape me. But I am pure by nature and successfully resisted him.[32] Even so, people thought I was his mistress.

"Because my friend was so busy carrying on with her husband, I had to take care of Master Inconstant who eventually grew up and married a woman of his mother's choosing, one Miss Unsteady.[33] His wife was a restless woman who pandered to her husband's every whim by assuming moods pleasing to him. Though he could fly hundreds of miles and return in a twinkling, he was completely restless and bored. His wife, [34] however, entertained him by endlessly creating exciting new situations, and becoming whatever he wanted so that

---

32. The seeming association of the pure Self with the ego. Ignorance causes the pure Self to seem ignorant, even though it is never actually contaminated.

33. The emotions.

34. The unholy alliance between the emotional and intellectual faculties in a person who has forgotten who they really are. In a Self realized soul the intellect, steeped in wisdom, maintains emotional stability but in an ordinary person the emotions, stirred by ignorance, eventually come to dominate the intellect causing one to behave irrationally.

he eventually fell completely under her spell. Shortly after their marriage they moved to the city of ten gates." [35]

"She bore him five devoted sons[36] who were also entrusted to my care. Each erected a splendid palace in which to entertain the father. In one he could listen to all manner of pleasant music: incantations of the Vedas, the reading of scriptures, the humming sounds of bees, and the twittering of birds. Sometimes he heard the raging sea, thunderclaps, earthquakes, the roar of lions, the rattle of the dead, and the lamentations of the living."

"In the second son's house which circulated hot and cold vapors, he experienced rock hard furniture and slept in a downy bed in silky pajamas. He was pleased with whatever felt good and displeased with whatever felt uncomfortable."

"When he visited the third son he saw innumerable scenes in immeasurable colors, some pleasing and some unpleasant."

---

35. The body.
36. The five senses.

"In the forth son's mansion he spent his days drinking sweet, sour, pungent and astringent liquids."

"In the last son's home he was treated to every imaginable smell."

"The sons were so devoted to their father they would not touch anything in their homes in his absence." [40]

"Master Inconstant, being inconstant, divorced Miss Unsteady and wedded Madame Vorax[41] whom he loved heart and soul. Madame Vorax had a huge belly and a very long pencil-thin neck. She kept her new husband and his five sons busy from dawn to dusk stocking in provisions...for she had a gargantuan appetite. All her men became weak and sickly from working to meet her needs. Yet, because her hungry belly was so large and her neck so long and narrow it took forever for small

---

40. A reference to the fact that sense information is useless unless a conscious being (the mind/intellect/ego entity) is connected to the senses. In deep sleep, some forms of meditation and intense internal concentration sense information is unavailable to the conscious being.
41. The principle of ignorance-born Desire. Voraciousness.

Tripura Rahasya

quantities of food to reach her stomach - no matter how much she ate. Therefore, she was always hungry. Eventually, she gave birth to two dear sons. The elder she named Master Flaming-Mouth[42] and the younger, Master Mean.[43] Alas, theirs was not a happy family because whenever Mr. Inconstant had sex with Madame Vorax, which was often, Master Flaming-Mouth scorched his body and Master Mean, a contemptuous fellow, beat him mercilessly.[44] Eventually Mr. Inconstant lost all his energy trying to satisfy Madame Vorax. The situation became so bad he could no longer feed her properly. Fortunately, his grandmother, Madame Ignorance, had an endless store of food which she happily contributed, much to the delight of Madame Vorax."

---

42. Anger.

43. Aggression. Anger leads to aggression.

44. When the mind lusts for objects it feels guilty because it unconsciously knows that it is setting itself up for disillusionment and frustration. Guilt leads to anger and agression.

45. The Self associated with a given mind/intellect entity. When the mind/intellect entity sleeps the Self remains awake. 'Watching' is a symbol for the ever-aware Self, often referred to as a 'witness.

46. Karma, activity. Karma, the momentum of past actions, is always at work, keeping the body alive even when we sleep. (over)

"When Master Inconstant fell asleep, watched by my friend,[45] his sons also fell asleep. On such occasions the city was guarded by his intimate friend, Mr. Motion,[46] who was continually moving to and fro by the upper gateway."

"During the interval between waking and sleep I would leave the city and remain in the blissful embrace of my Mother,[47] returning when Mr. Motion awakened his friend Mr. Inconstant."

"Mr. Inconstant and his sons could not live for a moment without Mr. Motion. Though only a seed he keeps the whole universe running. Smaller than the tiniest atom, he multiplies into all the names and forms we see here, sustaining and destroying everything. Like pearls in a necklace, he is the thread

---

46. (con't) Though apparently inactive when we sleep, it is actually generating the energy to wake us up, project the mind and unfold our lives. In its seed or causal state Karma is called the Causal Body because it causes the Subtle Body, the mind/intellect entity, to function. This is probably the reference to the "upper gateway."
47. When the mind/intellect sleeps the apparently limited Self shucks off its apparent limitations and 'merges' back into its original state. In fact, it was never separate. The letting go of its apparent limitation allows it to be what it is.

Tripura Rahasya

holding every experience together. He is the bond[48] between the prisoners in the city and myself. When the city has outlived its usefulness he spirits its citizens to another." [49]

"Though born of a virtuous mother, brought up by me and supported by such a powerful friend, Mr. Inconstant is always miserable. My friend, his mother, was stricken by grief by her son's calamities and nearly died of sorrow. I too suffered out of attachment to her. Indeed it seemed that I had become an ignorant, foolish, inconstant, unsteady, angry mean person, though I am always pure because I am one with my Mother, who is supremely good, subtler and more pervasive than space. She is all- knowing yet capable of limited knowledge. She is inactive yet capable of activity. Though unsupported and unattached, everything depends on her. Formless, she is all forms. Though illumining all she is unknown by any ego. She is bliss but not blissful. Though unborn and unmarried she has as many offspring as the ocean has waves. Like me, each is

---

48. Karma causes the association of the pure Self with the limited worlds.
49. Reincarnation

involved in the lives of his or her companions and yet possesses a secret inner knowledge that sets us apart from everything.[50]

"One day my friend became fed up with all the misery and asked the way out. I told her to divorce her husband, kill her son and imprison her grandchildren. Though she resisted at first, she soon saw the wisdom of my advice. When she had completed her tasks I introduced her to my Mother who embraced her with open arms.[51] She dived into the sea of Bliss and became Bliss itself.

"In the same way," Hemalekha concluded, "you can overcome your association with the unhealthy parts of yourself, transcend karmic propensities[52] and gain lasting happiness."

***

Hemachuda was astonished at his wife's tale. "I never know what to expect from you," he said. "No offense, but at times I think you are quite mad.

---

50. Self-Knowledge.
51. Self Realization doesn't happen until one's attachments are dissolved.
52. Conditioning.

I assume that you are not talking about reality because this is the second account of your past I have heard so far. I really do not know what to make of it."

"It is a fantastic story," said Hemalekha with great love, "and not to be taken literally. It is not about the 'reality' you are referring to but to an inner reality, a story going on all the time in every human being. I think I made a mistake assuming that you could relate to it at this point. Let us not worry about it now. I think it will make sense later when you have had more experience."

"You know, Hemalekha," I hate to say this, but I am not sure I like the way this relationship seems to be developing. It is very confusing. I never really know how to take what you say. Sometimes I think you are just using this whole spiritual idea to keep me down."

"I can understand how you must feel, since you have no way of verifying what I am saying. I guess you will just have to trust me. Perhaps we need to go back to the wedding night where this all started."

"I do not think that is a good idea," said Hemachuda. "That was a very painful evening."

"I say that because I think you do not realize that I was so frank with you because I love you. I want this marriage to work and I believe that it will only work if we can really get to know each other. I will not accept the traditional relationship where the wife lives in the shadow of the husband. I need to be appreciated for who I really am. Because you cannot always see that I need to show you."

"I know how hard it is to listen to a woman. But I am on your side. Part of you knows that because my words had such a powerful effect on you before. Try to find that part and hear me with an open mind."

Hemachuda made a determination to try.

She continued, "Everything in this world depends on trust. The farmer who plants crops trusts that sun and rain will bless them. Can a baby survive without trust in its mother? Or a lover gain pleasure without trust in his or her beloved? The universal belief that the law of cause and effect will produce certain results is based on trust. The order of nature and the very fabric of society depends on it.

"Yes, you need to trust me. I think trust will come if we work at it, but I do not fault you for not swallowing everything I say because right now you have no way of knowing what is behind it."

"But I think that no matter what happens with us, you have been deeply affected by what has happened and you will always look behind the surface to find the truth, so if you cannot trust me why not take scripture as your guide?"

"What scripture?" Hemachuda said.

"Our ancient texts. The Vedas and the Upanishads. They are saying what I am saying. And if you cannot trust them, trust the Lord because faith is always superior to cynicism."

As he listened Hemachuda's negativity slowly dissolved.

"I am sorry I doubted you," he said. "I seem to have been under the spell of Madame Ignorance. Your words have again awakened me again. I am so lucky to have met you. What should I do next?"

" After I have explained a teaching and you have taken it in you must follow up with appropriate effort. The path to Self-Realization is a path of self transformation. Intellectual understanding is very important...but not enough."

"And the very first thing - what you need to come back to over and over - is the realization that life without Self-Knowledge is suffering. If you are still trying to attain happiness in the world, like a relationship with me or anyone else, you are not ready for this excellent path. Next you need to see that if it were possible to get out of it on your own you would have escaped by now. You need help. But you cannot completely rely on a teacher either, so you need to appeal to the Creator. Without God's grace, spiritual progress is impossible. When God, is invoked with a pure heart, Self-Knowledge will come."

"What if I do not believe in a Creator?"

"Fair enough. But let me ask you this: who made you? If you say a sperm and an egg, who made the sperm and egg? If you say your parents, who made them? When you trace back you come to a point where you understand that something much greater than the sum of its parts had to make the universe. And it is that uncaused partless whole you need to invoke."

"If It has the power to generate this bewitching illusion, It also has the power to wake you up."

"So why doesn't It just wake me up and be done with it?"

"Because you have unconsciously been telling It you enjoy sleeping."

"How?"

"By taking the world to be real and trying to get happiness in it. Because It[53] created you free, It assumes that you have chosen to live the way you do. It is only when you are tired of the game of life

---

53. The original text used the masculine pronoun "He" because Consciousness, ordinarily symbolized as a male, is femine in this text. Vedic spiritual science generally sees creation as a union between two cosmic principles, Consciousness and energy (*shakti*) or Spirit and matter. Non-dual Vedanta does not admit a creation separate from the creator. But in so far as we take our interpretation of sense experience as real, the creation seems to be separate from the Creator. In this case Vedanta admits another principle, *Maya*. *Maya* is the misapprehension of a creation caused by the non-apprehension of the Self. But whether one accepts the dualist or non-dualist view, the Self is genderless.

that your mind changes. By getting to work spiritually, praying sincerely and working on yourself, you put the God on notice that you want out. Eventually He responds by lifting you out of the illusion, helping you transcend suffering. Then you realize that you were never bound, that you have always been free."

"If you have a problem with the idea of God, then put your trust in scripture. It also shows the way out."

"I do not know about this God idea," said Hemachuda. "The universe seems unintelligent to me. I think it is just matter."

"I do not want to argue with you," his wife said, "but scripture says that matter by definition is unintelligent and therefore incapable of conscious thought, feeling, and activity."

"If you argue that you are just matter, I wonder why a random accumulation of chemicals is so interested in the question of happiness. And on the larger scale, how could something that is not conscious organize itself into what is obviously a well-ordered and beautiful world?"

"Another argument to consider is why the Lord has been worshipped for untold ages. People do not continue a practice unless they derive benefit. The Lord's mercy is beyond doubt and because of it He is rightly famed. Has any individual commanded the love and respect of billions of souls over millions of years? Surrender to Him and He will show you how to proceed on your path."

"In everyday life people are benefited by getting the attention of a patron. Service born of ambition may achieve quick results, but devoted service without ulterior motive will eventually be appreciated. Though it takes humans a long time to recognize unmotivated activity, the Lord, who dwells in the hearts of all as the innermost Self, immediately bestows the appropriate fruits."

"Selfish devotees, those who use the Lord to satisfy desires for wealth, security, and pleasure need to wait to have their desires fulfilled. Those who want subtle things are more likely to get instant results."

"It seems this Lord you are talking about is quite unfair, distinguishing between one kind of devotee and another," replied Hemachuda.

"It may seem that way, but consider this. If a person prays for physical wealth, for example, which is a human creation, it has to come from the existing supply. In this world, desirers are many and desired objects few, so the Lord is constrained by limitations in the system. Since everyone is consciously or unconsciously praying for wealth and the existing wealth has been distributed according to the needs of the total, to immediately deprive one person to satisfy another is not only unfair but perverse. So the distribution of wealth depends on the scarcity principle established by human beings, not on God."

"On the other hand prayer for spiritual wealth, which is unlimited and your very nature, can be granted whenever one is truly ready to receive it. If your suffering is caused by an incorrect understanding of yourself it can be corrected at any moment. Therefore pray for enlightenment and enlightenment alone. Your prayers will surely be answered."

46   *Tripura Rahasya*

"Pure devotion transcends natural laws. Do you remember the wonderful story of the *rishi* Markandeya who did penance for a son?

When Shiva appeared and asked if he wanted a dull-witted boy who would live a long time or a brilliant boy who would die at sixteen, the *rishi* chose the latter.

Accordingly, a charming, dutiful, intelligent son was born. As he grew the parents became more and more sad. The son asked the reason and they told him of Shiva's conditions. He told them not to worry and undertook rigorous penance which pleased Shiva who ordained that the boy remain sixteen for all eternity." [54]

---

54. The text seems to contradict itself. Previously, Hemalekha said that God was bound by the laws operating in the creation. Now we're told that God can suspend the laws of the universe, in this case, time. Actually, time is only a concept, like the idea of scarcity, so it can be altered from within. What this means is that the parents can gain the vision of their son's true eternal nature and therefore not lament the demise of the body.

In fact, there are many examples in spirtual literature of the power of pure devotion (*para bhakti*) over natural law.

"Only the weak-minded believe they cannot escape their destiny. Even yogis, by purifying their *samkaras*,[55] can alter the course of their lives. If human beings can change their realities by proven methods, how difficult would it be for the ruler of the universe to alter your destiny?"

"Therefore, take refuge in the Lord. He will spontaneously take you to the goal."

"I am still not clear who the Lord is," Hemachuda said. Do you mean one of our Gods like Shiva, Vishnu, or Rama? The different sects and religions speak as if their's were the only one. Which is true? I am starting to believe that you really do know what you are talking about, that perhaps your father did enlighten you. Please teach me."

"The God I am talking about is the all-seeing, luminous, formless pure Consciousness that generates, permeates, sustains and destroys the universe. It is none of these deities and all of them. It is the one Being that many different religions and sects call by various names and worship in different ways. If you look into the root meanings of the many

---

55. Subconscious impressions, conditioning.

names of the deities you will see that each reveals something of the nature of the nameless Self. *Shiva* means 'that which is good under all conditions and at all times.' *Vishnu* means 'all-pervading.' Consciousness pervades everything just as space pervades all physical objects. *Rama* means 'the one who revels in the hearts of all.' The Self is the essence of everything."

"To think of the nameless and formless Spirit as if it were a God, like Shiva with three faces, three eyes, a blue neck, and a body smeared with ashes, one endowed with a body and mind, like us, is a projection of ignorance. Humans need instruments (bodies and minds) because we are not-self existent. Because of our limited capacities we assume Consciousness is like us."

"The non-dual Self, however, is whole and complete and needs no instruments to create the universe. Were instruments required they would have to be requisitioned from some other Being or another universe. The universe is created out the Self by Its own intelligence just as the spider's web is fashioned by its intelligence. What we see here, ourselves included, is just the Self sporting in an apparently dualistic universe."

"If it is non-dual why does it seem to be dual?" said Hemachuda.

"If you look at clear water in a colored glass the water seems colored. If you look at the universe through the ego, the apparently separate self, it seems to be dual. Transcend or temporarily remove the ego and duality disappears, revealing only pure Consciousness."

"This nameless, formless Being seems so abstract and inconceivable I have no idea how to relate to It," said Hemachuda. Please tell me how to worship It."

"Worship It in any form you wish," Hemalekha replied. "Because the Self is the knowing principle in your own mind, it understands your innermost desire and operates through your chosen deity to reveal Itself to you. As you worship your deity your mind becomes subtler and subtler, quieter and quieter, and at special moments dissolves into you, the worshipper - who is none other than the Self. At that point you find yourself to be beyond all forms, non-dual and eternally aware."

***

Dattareya paused, for his story was nearly finished. Then he continued.

"Hemalekha's words sent an inspired Hemachuda to his royal chambers where he lost himself in worship of the Goddess, very much as you did after I taught you the appropriate meditations. His craving for outer pleasure soon diminished and he settled into one-pointed investigation of the Self."

"How does investigation relate to meditation?" Parasurama asked.

"Meditation is the art of quieting the mind to produce transcendence," said Dattatreya. "Our sages discovered that when the waves in the mind are effaced, the Self shines in all its glory.[56] Very often,

---

56. This idea, the basis of *yoga*, comes from the Patanjali Yoga Sutras, a codification of yogic doctrines of great antiquity. The idea is not mentioned in the original text but is included by the author because it relevant to the topic of meditation.

when the Self is experienced the intellect is so stunned it is incapable of investigating the Self. When the experience ends, as does every experience, the meditator comes back to the normal waking state without clear knowledge...without having discovered that he or she is the Self. Identification with the ego is not broken and the old life resumes, full of pleasures and pains."

"Inquiry applies to both the normal and the transcendental situations. In the seat of meditation and in daily life the meditator objectifies and analyzes the content of the mind and negates it as 'not Self.' Dedicated application of this technique produces transcendence, experience of the Self. The Self, which is actually always experienced but seems hidden, becomes an obvious object of experience when identification with the three bodies and their respective objects are negated. If the discriminator/meditator continues to investigate the Self from the transcendental position, knowledge of the Self dawns. **Knowledge of the Self is not liberation because the Self is thought to be an object of experience.** But continued and intense investigation destroys the misconception that the Self is an object of experience, the final impediment to liberation. Liberation from the body, mind and intellect arises simultaneously with the knowledge that you are the Self. With knowledge that you are the Self, experience of the Self ceases. How can you experience yourself? You are yourself."

"When you talk about 'the transcendental position,' do you mean when you are beyond body/mind consciousness and seeing, as it were from the Self's position?" asked Parasurama.

"Yes. To understand that you must have meditated successfully," Dattatreya replied.

"The trick of meditation is to stay in that position, keep the mind quiet, and quietly observe your relationship to the body/mind and the world as it actually is. The longer you hold the mind on the Silence, the clearer it becomes."

"Let us return to the story now and see what happened to Hemachuda."

"After three months of intense meditation he went to see his wifely guru. She bowed to him, washed his feet and spoke lovingly."

"It is so good to see you. How are you? You have been neglecting me for a long time. You used to visit me daily, saying that a moment without me was an eternity. What happened? I have been very distraught."

"Do not play with me" he said. "I know you are beyond this silly emotional business. Nothing can shake you. I came to ask some questions."

"What do you want to know?" she said, pleased that he had overcome his infatuation and regained his inner strength.

"What is the real meaning of that story you told me about your 'life?' What do all those people represent? While investigating my Self I came across many of those characters in some form or other, but I am not sure how they all fit together. I think it will now be helpful to know more."

"I am pleased that you have received the grace of the Goddess," she said. "Dispassion will not arise without Her blessing. I will explain the inner meaning of the story."

"This is the story of the spirtual path, the fall from grace and ultimate redemption. The Mother is the pure Self, pure Consciousness, eternally luminous and free."

"When the Self apparently falls under the spell of Ignorance, It imagines itself as a separate, limited entity."

"How can this happen?" said Hemachuda. "My experience tells me that the Self can never become deluded or limited."

"You are right," Hemalekha said, "That is why I said 'apparently' and 'imagines.' It cannot, but seems to. And in this 'seeming' the world is born with all its limited beings striving for perfection. This is such a subtle point the intellect can never properly grasp it."

"Why?"

"Because Ignorance, *Maya*, happens before the intellect emerges out of Consciousness. She is its cause. And an effect, being gross, can never comprehend its cause. For example, Senses are aware of the Sense Objects but not aware of Mind. Mind is aware of the senses but not of Intellect. Intellect is aware of Mind but not of Self. Ignorance is sandwiched between Intellect and Self, subtler than Intellect but grosser than Self. So Intellect can never really understand Ignorance."

"This Ignorance causes the sense of separation from life and our feelings of inadequacy and limitation. When you feel incomplete and empty, Desire, Madame Vorax, arises. She is responsible for all your desires, angers and fears. Intellect, Master Inconstant, reacts to these desires and fears, cravings and aversions, by planning and scheming. Intellect is inconstant because it cannot distinguish what is real from what is unreal. Therefore it is forever changing course, taking up and abandoning projects. It believes that by getting certain things and avoiding others, the fears and desires torturing it will be laid to rest and happiness will come. Since its dreams and plans are based on ignorance of the fact that, as the Self, it is already whole and complete, they are out of harmony with reality and destined to fail."

"To make matters worse Intellect marries Miss Unsteady, the Mind. The Mind is responsible for the emotions and feelings. It enters into this alliance because successful action in the world, action calculated to get the objects and perform the activities meant to bring fulfillment, requires emotional power. But his bride is also ignorant of the pure Love that she is, and is therefore extremely unreliable, changing course, flitting from one thing to another like her husband."

"The emotions are the shock troops in the battle with life, moving the senses toward and away from the sense objects."

"When the senses act in the world motivated by a selfish, ignorant mind they create subconscious impressions that work out as *karma*, Mr. Motion. Karma forces the body/mind complex to behave habitually, sometimes compulsively. These habits reinforce existing subconscious tendencies and cause further *karma*. Before long one is completely caught up in one's rituals, repeating things over and over, until boredom and frustration threaten to destroy the personality."

"To free my friend, the embodied Self, from its dangerous liaison with Mr. Fool, the separated habituated ego, *karma* must be burned up. This is why I advise her to divorce her husband (dis-identify with the ego), kill her son (destroy false ideas) and imprison her grandchildren (keep her senses in check). Though a difficult process, she eventually accomplished this task and was ready for Self

The Mystery Beyond the Trinity

realization. Therefore, I introduced her to my Mother whom she embraced with open arms. She dived into the sea of Bliss and became Bliss itself."

"What a beautiful teaching," said Hemachuda. "Our ancient seers knew what they were talking about. How clearly they laid it all out, a whole science of life. And in such a humorous way. It is amazing that nobody thinks like this any more. And now it is even obvious to me. How fortunate I am! What have I been doing all my life?"

"Yes, it is the truth," Hemalekha said. "It was not as difficult for me because my father knew the truth. It just got into me by osmosis."

"The purpose of this teaching is to make you aware of the subtle forces that keep you bound to the wheel of *kama* and *karma*, Desire and Action. As you become more aware, misconceptions about yourself and the world disappear...making you fit for transcendence."

"I understand. I will work hard. I am sorry I doubted you. Until now I did not really realize who you are, but now things are very clear. Still, I would like to hear more about the Mother whose loving embrace is the goal of all our efforts."

Tripura Rahasya

"Listen carefully, dear." she said. "Your devotion to the truth has made your intellect capable of understanding. I will now impart the knowledge required for a successful investigation."

"My Mother is the Self. The Self cannot be objectified. Therefore it cannot be understood by the mind because the mind is only capable of understanding objects.[57] I cannot really tell you about It. Or when I do speak, you must understand that the words are not it, that they are simply meant to lead your mind in a certain direction."

"However, the Self exists in everyone and everything...so It can be known. You will not find It in the world of objects, even though all objects are illumined by It, because objects seemingly absorb Its light, making It unrecognizable. However, It shines brightly in a pure mind and can be realized there. For example, light shines equally on a mirror and the wall behind it, yet you see yourself only in the mirror because its surface is reflective. Therefore, purify your mind."

---

57. In Vedantic literature the word "object" refers to both physical and subtle objects. Subtle objects are mental (concepts and ideas) and emotional (feelings) phenomena.

"Asking me to show It to you is like asking me to show you your own eyes."

"Yes, said Hemachuda, "but sometimes I see It clearly when you speak. Perhaps I should just listen to you."

"That's good," Hemalekha replied, "But you need to free yourself of the *guru* too. You must find It on your own using the knowledge you have gained from me. Then It will be yours and yours alone. Listen attentively."

"As long as the intellect is contaminated by notions of 'I and mine, you will not find the Self. Listen to your speech. When you hear yourself saying 'I,' think about who is speaking. Is it you or is it the ego? Analyze your thoughts and see how many are 'I' related. For example, how do you think of me? Do you see me as 'your' wife or do you see me as your Self? Look at everything dear to you and try to see it as it is without 'I' and 'mine.' Let go of everything that you think of as 'mine.' When you are free of the push and pull of objects, see what is left. Every object, subtle and gross, can be discarded, but the one who discards them can never

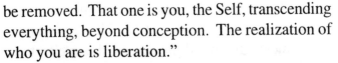

be removed. That one is you, the Self, transcending everything, beyond conception. The realization of who you are is liberation."

After receiving instructions Hemachuda entered a crystal palace in the royal pleasure garden outside the city, dismissed his attendants and climbed to a room on the ninth story with a panoramic view. He sat on a comfortable cushion and thought "How deluded I have been trying to find lasting happiness in objects for the sake of a Self that is already happy. Hemalekha is right. I need to discover the Self as it is, disassociated from everything.

Obviously my home, wealth, and wife are not me. Nor are they 'mine.' 'Mine' is just a concept, a social construct.

The body, which is composed of the five elements and always changing cannot be the eternal unchanging Self. It cannot be 'me' because I use it. It is therefore only a tool.

The mind and intellect are also constantly changing and limited in every way. In deep sleep they do not exist, yet I exist. Like the body, they are merely my tools.

"Furthermore, I am aware of the body and mind, yet they are unaware of me. The senses know the elements, the mind the senses, the intellect the mind, and the intellect? It must be known by the Self. So why is not the Self obvious? Because I am caught up in my perceptions, experiences, thoughts and feelings. The mind is the instrument that makes experience possible, so I will stop it and see what happens. If it is no more, the Self should manifest."

To his surprise he was able to bring his mind to a still point causing him to experience a vast emptiness. When the experience ended he was sure he had realized the Self.

He decided to repeat the meditation but this time he saw a blazing limitless light. When he came back to reality he was puzzled because the experience was quite different from the first.

The third meditation produced a deep sleep filled with wonderful dreams, further confusing him. "If the Self is non-dual," he thought, "why does it seem different every time I stop my mind?"

He stopped his mind a forth time, lost external awareness and experienced a state of deep bliss that went on for several days. The experience, which surpassed anything he could ever have imagined, was so powerful his previous meditations seemed trivial.

This caused him to wonder how he could experience bliss without the mind. "Hemalekha said all experience is dualistic, a transaction between a subject and an object," he thought to himself, "so what was experiencing the bliss?"

"I am confused. Which of these experiences is the Self? Or is the Self perhaps another experience? I need help."

He sent for his wife who discovered him sitting in meditation, a peaceful smile on his radiant face. "What can I do for you?" Hemalekha said, as she entered his chambers. "You seem quite happy. I take it you are working on yourself."

"Yes," he said, touching her feet and offering her a seat, "but I have some questions. Each time I meditated I experienced something different."

After recounting each experience in detail, he asked, "Which experience is the Self?"

"It is a good beginning," she said. "You will not make serious progress without meditation, but I need to tell you that none of these experiences is

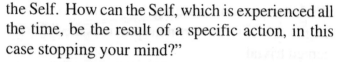

the Self. How can the Self, which is experienced all the time, be the result of a specific action, in this case stopping your mind?"

"Experienced all the time? What do you mean?" Hemachuda said. If it is experienced all the time, then everyone is enlightened. I do not get it."

"Everything is the Self," his wife replied. "The experiencer, the experienced, and the experiencing. It is not something in a special state, obtainable only through extreme means. Everyone is always enlightened; they just do not know what the Self is."

"I am not suggesting you stop meditating," she said, "but what can you do to get what you already have? If meditation is an act of mind, how will it produce the Self? Meditation is valuable in that it temporarily gets the mind out of the picture, but if you have to keep meditating to experience the Self, when will you have time to live your life?"

"The Self is always here, always available, the most essential and intimate part of every experience, with or without a controlled mind. You are always in the presence of the Self, continually experiencing it. Yet it remains 'apart' because you do not know what it is."

"One day a man found an interesting rock in a field. He took it to the marketplace and displayed it in his shop as a decoration. A jeweler noticed it and recognized it as an opal of immense value. The shopkeeper, thinking it was just an interesting rock, sold it for a pittance."

"Although the original owner experienced the rock, he did not know what he was experiencing, so he let it go for next to nothing. The second man experienced it too, but he knew what it was. Knowing was the only difference. And what a difference that is!"

Hemachuda responded, "You seem to be saying that trying to get a particular experience of the Self through meditation is not the way to go. Should I continue meditating?" said Hemachuda.

"By all means," his wife replied. "Meditation turns the mind in the right direction. The next time you meditate in this way, pay attention to the short interval between the last thought and the experience of light or darkness or bliss. If your mind is subtle enough you can recognize the Self there as effortless awareness. The Self is difficult to recognize because the mind is extroverted. Even the experience of the darkness, the light, and bliss are 'outer' experiences to the Self, though they seem to be 'inner' experiences to you."

"And secondly, if you find the gap, and a mystic experience occurs, ask yourself how you know this experience. Meditation experiences are like waking dreams. In sleeping dreams you see many things, yet your eyes are completely non-functioning. In what light are these subtle events taking place? Though physical light is absent, you can see quite clearly. The light illumining them is the Self, just as the Self illumines your mystic experiences."

"The Self is like the light rays coming from the sun. You cannot see the rays themselves but they are capable of illumining objects. This Self, effortless awareness, is very difficult to grasp. The more you try to see It the more It eludes you, like trying to step on your own shadow. When you look at yourself in a mirror you are so concentrated on your image that you do not see the mirror. Similarly, concentration on your thoughts, feelings, and perceptions reduces your natural panoramic awareness to a fine shaft and causes you to miss the

66

light in which your perceptions are taking place. Just as people do not notice space because of their fixation on the objects in space, the Self is unknown because of your fixation on experience."

"Reality consists of a Seer and the seen, Consciousness and objects. The objects perceived by the senses, mind, and intellect are the non-Self. The Self, which is often called the Knower, is self-known. Objects like the senses and mind (which are just material instruments) cannot validate Its existence."

"That does not make sense," Hemachuda said obviously puzzled. "You mean the eyes do not see the world, the ears do not hear sounds? I cannot accept that."

"It is understandable that you should make this mistake," relied Hemalekha, "but if the eye is what is seeing, then it would see when removed from the body - but it does not. The senses and mind are just instruments, like a telescope, through which Consciousness sees. Take away any object in Consciousness' panoramic field and Consciousness, the Seer, is unaffected. But if you were to take away Consciousness, which, of course, you cannot, there would be no objects. Everything in your world depends on the fact that you are a conscious being. Consciousness, not Hemachuda, is you. Hemachuda is little more than a bundle of subtle tendencies illumined by you."

"When the Knower cognizes an object through an instrument, knowledge arises. Knowledge is not possible without the Knower. Think of it like this: objects and knowledge are only reflections in eternal, self-luminous, Consciousness - the Knower. If you were to dissolve every object in the universe, the Knower, you, would be left over. Try to dissolve yourself. It is impossible. You are permanent and unchanging. You are whole and complete, not subject to validation or removal."

"When you identify yourself as the Knower of the restless mind you are free because you cannot be what you perceive."

"But I thought the Self was all the objects too," Hemachuda said. "If it is non-dual, then the objects have to be the Self, just as the waves are also the ocean."

"Very good!" Hemalekha said, "You are definitely thinking clearly. But this vision only comes after you negate the objects as not-Self. Negation of the objects separates the gross and subtle manifestations of Consciousness from Consciousness itself. When Consciousness is realized in its unmanifest state and all confusion of it with objects is laid to rest, you are completely free. Then you will understand the magic by which Consciousness appears as objects which is similar to the way water assumes the shapes of the earth into which it flows. The mere intellectual understanding that everything is non-dual Awareness is not liberation because suffering continues. Your inquiry is over when your sense of limitation disappears."

"Are there other meditations that might reveal the Self?" Hemachuda asked.

"Indeed." his wife replied. "Keep your mind as quiet as possible. Stay away from all distractions and become aware of the state between the waking and dream states. If you can let the mind empty without falling asleep you will recognize the Self in the space between waking and sleep."

"Notice the interval between the cognition of one object or event and another. One's life is so full that the mind hops from one event to another, from one thing to another, from the past to the present to the future without ever looking into itself. Keep the mind steady and indrawn and observe the interval between experiences."

"In this 'space' the Self, the substrate of the Universe, sits.[58] Identify with it and free yourself from sorrow. As the Self you will see that Hemachuda and all the objects in his world are only reflections of the mind. In the Self there are no senses or mind, nothing to be gained or realized. Finally, when you investigate the Self remember that you are what you are seeking."

"Bring the mind into the state of a newborn baby until you feel that you are separate from all objects and only the feeling of "I am" remains. Remain like that for a short time as if you were a blind man who came into a new room and was trying to 'feel' where each piece of furniture was situated.

---

58. The Self can obviously not 'sit' in any space. It is the awareness of space and space itself.

Then allow the feeling of 'I am' or 'I see' to dissolve. The Self transcends even this subtle feeling of being or witnessing."

"I think I have given you enough to work with so I will take my leave. I will come back in a few days to see how you are doing."

Hemachuda thanked her, touched her feet and showed her to the door. He immediately returned to his seat, closed his eyes and began to meditate.

When Hemalekha returned a few days later she found him sitting in deep meditation on the Self. Her arrival jarred him out of his state and irritated him.

"Perhaps you can come back another time," he said, closing his eyes. "I want to go back into that incredibly blissful state."

"I would not think of disturbing your meditation, but please quickly tell me what is the difference in your experience when your eyes are open or closed," Hemalekha replied.

On being pressed for an answer Hemachuda said, "Thanks to you I have discovered pure happiness. Worldly activities, including speech, give me no pleasure. I am through with them. I only

The Mystery Beyond the Trinity

want to sink into the ocean of bliss within. Perhaps you can leave now and let me return to the experience of that wonderful state. I am sorry to be so rude but that is all I want. And, to be truthful, I am surprised that you, who claim to know about this state, are not actually in it. Anyone not in it is wasting time."

"Hemalekha looked at her husband with amusement and replied, "So now you have become a guru. It sometimes happens that a disciple surpasses his or her guru. This is very interesting. Before I start to take instruction from you, however, please consider what I have to say."

"Very well," said Hemachuda with condescension.

"If your experience of the Self depends on whether or not your eyes are open or closed, how can it be enlightenment? The scriptures say that enlightenment is the knowledge that you are whole and complete Consciousness. Are you incomplete and unconscious when your eyes are open and complete and conscious when they are closed? How is it that your blissful nature stops being blissful when your eyes are open? How can such a trivial action deny you your own ever-present nature? Does it not seem a bit illogical that the movement of an eyelid an inch long can obscure the vastness in which the whole universe rests?"

"Secondly, the scriptures say the Self pervades everything, like space pervades all objects. When you close your eyes and return to it, just where do you go? If you are not seeing it here and now with your eyes open, there is something wrong."

"Thirdly, how can you be 'in' it? The scriptures say you are it. How can you be in or out of yourself? This is not possible."

"Finally, only fools think that liberation is an 'experience' of the Self. First, if experience of the Self were enlightenment, everyone would be liberated because all experience is nothing but the Self. How can it be otherwise in a non-dual universe? Second, if the experience of the Self were liberation then it would be a dualistic state, yet the scriptures say enlightenment is non-dual knowledge. Is it that you remain Hemachuda and add a special experience of overwhelming bliss to your self when you close your eyes and meditate? If that is what happens, then you have to be something other than the all-pervading non-dual Self. The Self is literally everything that is. There is nothing other than It to experience It. Your problem is that you have not 'experienced' It enough to have discovered that you are It."

"The concepts 'experience,' 'within and without,' 'in and out,' 'Self and not-self,' are useful when you do not know who you are. They point you in the right direction and help you distinguish the pure Self from Its many forms. This is indeed a high stage, but I suggest that you return to your meditation and continue to inquire until you no longer see the Self as an object.

"Do not worry, you will not lose your individuality forever. It will return purified and beautified from your journey. But you need to melt into the Self until the first thought in your mind is 'I am this.' Right now you are thinking of the Self as an object...'that.' When you are liberated your thought will be 'I am' and there will be nothing else to experience."

Overwhelmed by his wife's clarity and wisdom, Hemachuda once again realized he had more to learn.

"I am sorry I spoke so foolishly," he said. "I cannot argue with what you say and will use the information you have so graciously given to erase my false concepts. I can see that I am still identified with my body and my ego."

"You have taken in my words" Hemalekha replied. "Return to your meditation and you will be successful," she said with great love. "And then we will have truly attained oneness with each other."

Hemachuda did as instructed. After many months of investigation, one day while sitting on his royal bed meditating , he became aware that he was no longer Hemachuda meditating on the Self but that he was the Self looking out at Itself in the form of Hemachuda meditating, knowledge that never left him.

He left his meditation room and rejoined Hemalekha who was overjoyed to see him. And from this point on he had no complaints about her love.

With a perfectly-balanced mind he ruled his subjects fairly. The kingdom prospered and he set up schools that taught meditation and the knowledge of the Self to everyone.

Even his family, who wondered if he had gone mad when he took up with Hemalekha, noticed that he remained the same in pleasure and pain, was indifferent to loss and gain, treated friend and foe alike, undertook his royal duties like an actor in a play and was always happy.

One day when they asked him what was happening he told them about the Self. They were inspired to hear more, took him as a teacher, and eventually became liberated. The state ministers followed suit. Before long ordinary citizens began meditating and in a few years the whole city was enlightened. Even children and the aged were no longer moved by selfishness.

Everyone slowly became respectful of each other and lived in harmony with nature. Mothers sang lullabies of the Self to their babies. Masters and servants saw the Self in each other. Craftsmen built meditation halls and artisans fashioned symbols of the Self. Musicians chanted holy texts about Self realization and actors engaged in dramas depicting the war between the Self and the ego. Even the prostitutes treated their customers with real love and never overcharged for their services.

Nobody regretted the past or worried about the future. Everyone was quite happy with life as it unfolded and kept their minds focused on the Self, thus dissipating their latent tendencies.

The sages called theirs the City of Wisdom and visited it often. Even the parrots in their cages made profound statements like, "Meditate on the Self which is Pure Intelligence bereft of all objects of knowledge." Or, "What is known is not different from the Knower, Pure Intelligence." And, "The universe is like infinite images reflected in the mirror of absolute Consciousness." Some said, "The all-pervasive and limitless Consciousness is both the sentient and the insentient, the changing and the changeless. Those especially loquacious and gifted in logic said, "Everything is known by Intelligence but nothing knows It. Therefore let sensible people who are desirous of liberation give up the quest for intellectual knowledge and rediscover their own absolute Intelligence."

"So you see, Parasurama," Dattatreya continued, "the primary cause of liberation is association with the wise."

The End

Glossary

avadhut   The highest class of *sannyasins*, renunciates. *Avadhuts* are completely devoid of body consciousness. They are 'sky clad,' naked, have no fixed abode and do not beg for food.

bhakti   Devotion. There are two types of devotion: *guna* (conditioned) *bhakti* and *para* (pure) *bhakti*. Conditioned *bhakti* is devotion conditioned by one's psychological complexion. Unconditioned *bhakti* is pure love without qualifications. It is complete identification with the beloved.

brahmin   The religious or spiritual class. Those devoted to following and propagating *dharma*. Nowdays, the highest social caste, an hereditary designation.

dharma   The eternal way. Righteousness. A code of conduct and way of life based on universal values. The duties enjoined on a seeker.

adharma   Going against *dharma*. Actions motivated by selfish craving and fear.

Hanuman   The monkey God. A symbol of pure *bhakti*, unconditional love.

karma   Action. Activity. The results of action.

kshetriya   The military and political class. Those devoted to protecting *dharma* and the spiritual class.

mahatma   A great (*mahan*) soul (*atma*). Mahatmas are Self-Realized beings.

om   A symbol of the Self, pure consciousness.

Pauranas   The mythic literature that characterizes Vedic culture. The Pauranas enshrine Vedic ideas and ideals in charming stories and tales of the deeds and exploits of the Gods.

Rama   'The one who revels in the Heart.' A great king, an incarnation of Vishnu, the Self. The protagoist in the Ramayana, one of Vedic culture's two major epics.

rishi   A seer. The spiritual visions of the *rishis* are the basis of Vedic culture. A sage.

sanskrit   'Well-done, purified.' A revealed spiritual language. The language of the Vedas.

shabda   Sound. Words. The oral means of teaching Self knowledge.

shastras   Scriptures. Vedic texts containing the science of Self-Knowledge. The Upanishads, the Bhagavad Gita, the Puranas, Yoga texts, etc.

Shiva   'That which is good at all times and places.' A word describing the Self. A Pauranic diety. Shiva is an ascetic, a meditator.

Self   The essence of everything. Pure Consciousness. The holy Spirit. The source of lasting happiness. The object of all striving.

tapas   'Heat-producing." Any discipline, including meditaton, that generates energy. Ascetic practices.

tripura   'Three cities.' The three states of consciousness: waking, dream, and deep sleep.

upasanas   The rituals and meditations enshrined in the karmic portion of the Vedas.

upanishads   The portions of the Vedas containing the visions of the *rishis* which have been subsequently developed into Vedanta, the 'science' or way to the Self. Their fundamental idea, that the whole universe is spirit or pure consciousness, is the basis of Vedic culture.

Vedas   *Veda* means knowledge. The Vedas are voluminous texts of great antiquity that contain both the religious and spiritual ideas of the Hindus. The Vedas are composed of two sections. The section on karma details the actions necessary to obtain desireable objects in this lfe and the hereafter. The section on knowledge is called the Upanishads and is the source of the Vedanta.

Vedanta   Literally, *veda anta*, the end of the Vedas. Also, the knowledge (*veda*) that ends (*anta*) the search for knowledge, or Self-Knowledge. Vedanta is a means of Self knowledge. It is an oral tradition that stretches back thousands of years to Vedic times.

vichara   Inquiry, investigation. Vichara is a rigorous method of inquiring into the Self.

vishnu   'All-pervading.' A word describing the Self. A Pauranic diety, the 'long strider.' One of the three universal principles operating in the manifest realm.

yoga   To yoke, join. The union of the individual soul with the Self, the universal Spirit. One of the two main Vedic spiritual traditions, the other being Vedanta. A path of purification and experience of the Self.